CHAPTER 1

It was a cold wintry night. The wind was howling, danced as the wind whistled through them. The lig to pulse as wave after wave of rain fell. The desen the rain showed no sign of stopping.

The ferocity of the weather matched only by the fer⌐⌐.⌐y ⌐⌐⌐ied in the face of a killer, gripping his victims throat tighter and tighter. She tried to kick but couldn't free herself from the cord that bound her ankles tight to the frame of the bed. She tried to scream but every time she tried to breathe her underwear, this sadistic bastard stuffed in her throat, was becoming more lodged. She looked into his eyes and saw his pupils were dilated. He had a strained look on his face. He was enjoying this. She fought as hard as she could. She could feel her life ebbing away.

She summoned all her energy for a final effort to free herself, trying to ignore the excruciating pain in her right hand, where he had cut off her fingers using a pair of secateurs. But she was no match for the powerful maniacal beast brutally squeezing the life out of her. She felt him continuing to thrust himself into her while she lay there. What had she done to deserve this? She looked towards the door in a final look of hope that someone would burst through it….. She took her last breath.

When he finished, he climbed off her and sat looking at her motionless body. A sense of achievement overwhelmed him. He'd done it, after all these years. His first kill. The more he thought of it, the more excited he became.

He buttoned up his shirt, looked over to her lifeless body and smiled. He picked up her fingers, the secateurs and put them in his kit bag containing what he felt were the necessary tools to do his work. Hammer, saw, pliers, secateurs, rope, tape, balaclava, stun gun and an assortment of knives. He calmly put his jacket, hat and gloves on, before picking up his bag, switching the light off as he left.

DCI MARKS

The alarm clock rang at the usual time (half past five) for Detective Chief Inspector Conor Marks. Is it that time already he thought?

A sigh of resignation. Why had he chosen a career that seemed to allow him little or no sleep on such a regular basis. If I knew then what I know now he thought, I'd have become a librarian or something. Anything other than a Police Officer. Getting up early for Detective Chief Inspector Conor Marks every day had started to take its toll on him. Lately he was constantly feeling tired. He was getting as much sleep as he normally was but for some reason it didn't seem enough anymore. Maybe time was taking its toll on him, maybe all the days, nights, weeks of getting by on 3 hours of sleep here and 3 hours of sleep there were finally catching up with him.

He could still remember the days when he played football for hours with his mates. Now even the thought of it left him feeling exhausted.

He stumbled to the bathroom. He turned the tap on. The ice-cold water he splashed on his face woke him up.

A look in the shaving mirror quickly reminded him how old he was looking. Gone was the fresh faced smiling wide-eyed young boy, replaced by a wrinkled older man with greying hair whose eyes had seen some horrific sights in the last 25 years.

He'd been feeling extremely tired of late, struggling to focus on work, and lacking in motivation. This was very unusual for him. He had wanted to be a police officer since he was a boy. Motivation was something he never lacked.

He had been receiving several letters a week from the local hospital asking him to attend at the hospital on this date and time, only for him to arrange to get the time off, then get another letter saying the date and time had been changed.

However, after having several scans and tests done, he had an appointment with a Consultant Neurologist. About 6 months ago Marks had begun to feel as if his left elbow was being weighted down. Simple movements were getting harder every day. He had gone to the doctors and was told that he believed it was Carpal Tunnel Syndrome but that he would have to undergo tests to confirm this.

He'd had a brain scan recently whereby he had to lie down whilst the machine moved around your head taken pictures of your brain. At least they let you wear headphones and listen to music. They had a collection of cd's to choose from. The machine took around thirty minutes to do what it was meant to do. He chose the Beatles, because, well, why wouldn't you? Their music was quite simply the best.

When the machine had finished, he tried to ask the radiographer if everything looked fine but got the standard response that his doctor would inform him soon enough.

Two days later he received a letter from the hospital stating he had an appointment to see Dr Harris, Consultant Neurologist in a few weeks. Finally, he'd find out what was wrong with his arm.

He returned to the bedroom and got dressed in the clothes he had set out the night before.

He made his way downstairs. The house was roasting. He forgot to change the time on the heating again. He intended to have a quick cup of coffee before he left but would you believe it, the kettle wasn't working. Shit. Hope this isn't a sign of things to come he thought. He grabbed his car keys and left for work.

He parked his car in his designated space. (A privilege of being the Detective Chief Inspector. It was like Wacky races at times trying to get a parking space at HQ such was the extent that police officers were now in desk jobs). Parking at Headquarters had become so bad that last week he saw one young officer sitting in his car eating his breakfast cereal from a tupperware box, just to avoid paying for parking at the adjacent multi-storey car park.

He got out of the car, unsure how he managed to arrive at the station as he couldn't remember driving to work such was the familiarity of the journey. This compounded by the million and one things in his mind he had to contend with that day.

'Morning sir,' said the constable, clearly still young enough to have energy at that time of morning despite the fact he was obviously part of the night shift.

'Morning' he replied. Looking at the constable whilst thinking, I can remember being that enthusiastic, having that drive. That brought a smile to his face, even though he wasn't a morning person, especially when he hadn't had a coffee to kick start his day.

The morning was hectic, as was every Monday. Marks had to sit in on the morning meeting. This meeting consisted of all the senior officers from various departments gathered every Monday to discuss what incidents occurred over the weekend. They discussed how the incidents were dealt with, how best to progress with them, who was arrested, if there were any road traffic incidents and if there are any vulnerable missing persons.

The meeting was chaired by the Forces' Chief Superintendent.

This meeting was about information sharing and trying to promote an intelligence led police force which would enable them to utilise their resources to their maximum potential.

Although there was the usual weekend stuff, Domestic Assaults, assaults, thefts, drunken behaviour, a couple of indecent assaults and drugs offences, they had to discuss.

There were no major car accidents, or vulnerable missing persons so at least that was good.

Marks hadn't upset anyone so far, which was rare for him given his blunt, but honest replies when asked questions. He also managed to grab a bacon roll and coffee for his breakfast which was something of a rarity. He had become used to surviving on coffee and fresh air.

He was in his office doing paperwork which was the norm for him. Over the years he'd seen the job change a great deal. Whilst there had always been an element of paperwork, he thought police officers are not as visible on the street as much as they used to be because of the amount of paperwork involved in the job now.

He thought this was probably due to the police having to be more accountable for their actions. Especially in the age of social media where everyone has a mobile phone, and filming incidents as they're ongoing was commonplace. Officers needed to justify their role. He wasn't blaming the officers, after all, they were doing what they had been asked to do.

Marks thought they should get more police on the beat, get them speaking to the locals. Let them see the friendly face of the police because the way things have been for a while now, is that people only see the police when they are arresting someone. The locals do not know the officers who police their areas names.

When Marks was a young constable, he knew all the shopkeepers by name, and they all knew him. This built up a level of trust between the public which helped cut crime.

CHAPTER 2

Marks was sitting in his office when his phone rung, 'DCI Marks'
'Sir, it's Sgt Martin from the control room. There's been a murder'.

He noted the details and made his way to the Detective Superintendent's office. He was reaching the door as the DS was opening it. 'I was just on my way to see you Conor. There's been a murder in Kings Avenue.'
'That's what I was coming to see you about.' said Marks.
'We'll go to the incident room and talk there. Conor you'll be the SIO (Senior Investigating Officer) in this murder investigation and John (Thompson – Detective Inspector) will be your deputy, but, as usual, keep me informed of the progress of the enquiry.'

Within minutes the room was full of detectives.

The locus (scene where incident took place) was 64 Kings Avenue, Dundee. This was a building containing 12 flats in the richest area of Dundee. An unusual place for a murder in Dundee.

Single, white female killed in her own home. That was all they knew at this time.

Tasks were designated to the Detective Inspectors and uniformed inspectors, who would then assign them to specific officers. As new information was coming in all the time, the priority of the tasks changed frequently. Senior officers would have to supply the incident room clerical staff with the names and numbers of the officers assisting with this enquiry and the tasks they've been asked to do. All the tasks would then be submitted to HOLMES. This is the computer system used by police forces throughout Britain for major incidents. HOLMES – Home Office Large Major Enquiry System.

The Crime Scene Manager (CSM) Detective Sergeant James Budd was already on the scene. Marks liked Budd. He thought he was a very good cop and a very good Crime Scene Manager, a role he was experienced in. He had already locked down the scene. No one in or out unless approved by him.

When you must prove beyond a reasonable doubt that a person is guilty of killing someone, its imperative that you ensure the crime scene is as it was when the killer left. This means minimising the chances of anyone willingly or inadvertently contaminating the crime scene.

In order to do this Budd only allowed essential personal in the confines of the crime scene. He believed that only the victim, the killer, the unfortunate soul who found deceased, (In this case deceased's friend- Sharon Edwards) and the two officers who were called to the scene had been in this crime scene.

There was no need to call for an ambulance because it was established by the officers who were first on the scene that deceased had been dead for some time. (At least a day)

They (CSM and photographer/videographer – DC Martin) entered the flat once they had put their forensic suits on over their clothing. They defined a common approach path (this is the route determined by the CSM to the victim which minimises the disruption of the scene thus preserving evidence). Once this had been established, they entered the flat. Filming the scene as they went further and further into the crime scene.

Martin worked with Budd that often in crime scenes you could be excused for thinking he was the CSM such was his knowledge of what to do and what not to do.

The crime scene is filmed so that there is no dubiety as to where deceased was, where items were in relation to deceased, including blood, footprints and fingerprints.

Budd, using special equipment, looked to see if he could identify areas where the killer had left footprints, (regardless if its carpet or flooring, footprints can still be uplifted). He placed metal foot plates on these areas in order to protect the evidence. They would obtain casts/photos of these footprints when they were ready to. They may be lucky and get the killers footprint and if they're lucky they may find something unusual about the footprint thought Budd. Such as a cut in the sole or an obscure pattern.

Budd had previously found a footprint made by an offender's trainer in the mud outside of a house that had been broken into. He discovered there was a cut at the front of the trainer about an inch in length. Ten minutes after he arrived at locus, he was informed that uniformed officers had traced a well-known housebreaker nearby.

Aware of Budd's find, they checked his trainers. There was a cut in his trainer that was about an inch in length. That not only resulted in an arrest but a conviction at court.

The male received a 12-month jail sentence. Result.

Any persons who have entered the crime scene may, be required to have casts made of the soles of their footwear to eliminate them from any they may have obtained. This includes police officers.

Budd was speaking as Martin filmed. Wooden flooring in the hall that had a door to the left, which was a cupboard and the living room door to the right. Through the living room, walking on wooden flooring that had rugs about 2 inches thick on them. He noted that nothing appeared to be disturbed in the living room. It was like one of those houses you see in fantasy homes thought Budd.

Everything was immaculate. No expense had been spared on furnishings here. They reached the bedroom, having entered another smaller hall that led to the bedrooms and bathroom.

Martin continued filming. Clothes strewn across the room. Deceased lying naked on the bed, her wrists tied to the bed frame with cord. Her fingers on her right hand missing, her left hand intact.

Her ankles tied to the bed frame with cord. Budd noticed the cord was thin but strong. Deceased had obviously struggled for her life to the point where the cord had begun to cut into her wrists and ankles.

Deceased lay there staring into space, blood had seeped from her nose, her neck badly marked where the killer had squeezed the life out of her. They finished filming and left deceased's body where it lay. There was no need to remove the body quickly, they would keep it there until they gave themselves every chance of obtaining every ounce of forensic evidence.

At one point they had deceased's face and neck covered with forensic tape. This tape, allowed Scenes of Crimes Officers (SOCO's) to try and obtain the killers DNA from the victim. The killer most probably strangled deceased with his bare hands. If this was the case, then the secretion of sweat from the killer may have left DNA on the deceased.

Budd and Martin took deceased's clothes for forensic examination. On doing this they noticed deceased's underwear was missing. They thought that the killer must have taken these.

DS Black, who rarely stepped out of Headquarters these days due to the various meetings he has, had arrived at the scene with Marks.

56 – 78 Kings Avenue. It was a grand building, big and it only had 12 flats in it thought Marks. 'There's no hiding money, how much do you reckon these flats go for?' he asked Black.
'Half a million maybe', came the reply.
'I'm in the wrong job obviously' he said.

Marks received a call, it was Dr Lynne Dempster, the Police Forces' pathologist. She was arriving in the street.

Marks and Black got out of their car and greeted Dr Dempster. 'Good morning Lynne. How are you this morning?' said Marks.
'I'm fine. How are you gentlemen today?' she replied.
'Fantastic' said Marks sarcastically.
'Fine' replied Black.

'Shall we' said Dempster.

They walked up the stairs to entrance to the building where the uniformed Police Constable was standing with the Crime Scene Log. Although it was a secure entry system to the building, accessed by a security code, only the residents were supposed to know, access could also be granted by a concierge who is located at a central office. (The security firm oversees the security to several buildings throughout the city owned by different organisations).

He watches the cctv footage and grants the residents access if they've forgotten their key. If he doesn't know the persons at the door, he must call the person they claim to be visiting to confirm this, in order to let the person in.

Occasionally if a person isn't granted access and they manage to gain access, by either pressing another buzzer, or being granted entry by a resident. They may wait until someone else comes along and enters the building, and sneak in behind them. Then the concierge must inform their mobile security team, who will then attend the building and try to locate the person.

This was common policy in plush apartment blocks. Even the postman had to buzz the concierge to be allowed entry.

The police however, being present were making sure that even residents had to prove they resided in the building. This included people who lived below the victim.

They walked up the communal stairwell. For Marks it was easy seeing this was full of flats owned by people who took pride in where they stayed.

In Marks' first post he was assigned to work in the Hilltown area of Dundee. Not one of Dundee's more affluent areas. Some of the stairwells in the buildings he'd been in had graffiti on the walls, there was litter lying about and sometimes even used syringes. Due to some of the local drugs addicts injecting themselves, having just bought their drugs from a resident, unable to make it to home before the took their 'medicine'.

Marks and Black walked up to the flat, whilst Dr Dempster, who would admit she wasn't as fit as she should be, took the lift.

They were greeted by a depressed looking Constable. (Like every beat officer – probably got a hundred things to do, some of which he planned to get through today, until he was told to stand guard at a flat) 'Can you sign in please?' he said reluctantly. All too aware he was asking senior officers to do this.

'Of course,' said all three before signing the Crime Scene Log.

Before they entered all three got suited up into Forensic suits which went over their own clothes.

This included their shoes, which were covered with paper shoes, like ones you get at the swimming, stretchable paper ones though. These are worn to protect the scene from anything that could potentially ruin the chances of obtaining DNA.

When Budd was finished, he came out and met DS Black, DCI Marks and Dr Dempster, (the force pathologist) into the scene. Although they were his senior officers in rank, he was the Crime Scene Manager. He was in control of who came and went from the crime scene irrespective of rank.

'Morning sirs, morning doctor'

'Morning Jimmy' they both said.

'Good morning Jimmy' said the doctor.

'I believe the deceased is an Elaine Dawson, what do we know about her?' asked Marks.

Budd replied 'She's 32, single, lawyer, not surprisingly she is not known to us. All we know now, is that she left work about 5pm on Friday 1st March and wasn't seen or heard from until she was found this morning (Monday 4th March) around 0930 hours.'

'Who found her?' asked Black. They entered the bedroom and saw deceased lying on the bed naked, head to one side, blood coming out of her nose, no fingers on her right hand, her wrists tied to the bed frame, with cord, and the bed drenched in blood where her right hand fingers had been.

It appeared to them that she had her fingers cut off where she lay because there was blood spray on the wall behind her hand. Compression marks clearly evident on her neck. There was no blood trail anywhere else except for on the bed.

Budd spoke as Marks and Black inspected the scene. 'A co-worker, Sharon Edwards. She said staff at work were concerned for deceased because she hadn't turned up for an important meeting at work this morning.

She couldn't get a reply at the door, but she had a key from when she was house sitting for deceased when she was on holiday. She let herself in and found the deceased in her room. She phoned police but, yet, we haven't been able to note a statement from her, she's in shock'.

'The last confirmed sighting of her was Friday 5pm, when she left work.' added Budd.

Dr Dempster began to examine the body. She said she was almost certain strangulation was the cause of death but would confirm that when the post-mortem was carried out. She also discovered deceased appeared to have a burn mark on her shoulder. Marks and Black thought it could have been caused by a taser or a stun gun as it didn't look like a cigarette burn. It looked like she'd been bitten by a snake such was the size of the burn mark and their closeness to one another.

'This could explain how he managed to gain entry into the flat and control her. Doesn't explain why she opened the door though. Maybe she knew the person' said Black.

'The killer could have had a key' replied Budd.

Marks also thought that it may also indicate to them that this was pre-meditated. Maybe he knew her, watched her, knew she lived alone and knew it would be at least a couple of days before she was discovered, allowing him all the time he needed to murder her.

The doctor said deceased's fingers on her right hand were cut off whilst she was still alive.

She also indicated that judging by the temperature of deceased, that she had been dead for roughly two days, but couldn't be more specific because of the warmth of the house. Marks knew the body temperature decreases by roughly 1 degree centigrade an hour after death out in the open but in a house where the heating comes on and off its more difficult to estimate the time of death.

Marks noted deceased's clothes on the floor. They would be taken and submitted for DNA. They noted however, that deceased's underwear was missing. Like Budd and Martin, they concluded the killer had taken them. An expensive watch and a jewellery box, containing gold bracelets, necklaces and a few rings, sat on the dresser, quite clearly robbery wasn't the motive.

'Why cut the fingers off' said Marks, thinking out loud.
'Eliminate DNA from under her nails or maybe he keeps them as trophies. Some killers like to keep trophies of their victims' replied Dr Dempster. 'Ed Gein – the inspiration behind Silence of the Lambs character Buffalo Bill kept his victims skin, to make masks and bones to make furniture. Ted Bundy kept victims' heads. Jeffrey Dahmer kept his victim's heads and genitals as souvenirs. I can go on its fascinating....' said Dempster....

Before being cut short by Marks who said, 'That's fine thanks doctor'.

The last thing Marks needed was an enthusiastic serial killer fan happily telling him how some sick minded, psychopath ate his victims. Not that he was squeamish, it was just that the doctor seemed too pleased to be speaking about serial killers with an admiration for them, which he couldn't understand. He thought that we (society) have a fascination with killers and people like to know the serial killers name, his modus operandi (Way of working), how many victims, across what time period etc. Yet, he was willing to bet big on this, most people couldn't name one or more of the killers' victims.

"Let's see if we can get DNA off something. We'll need to get someone to make enquiry with the hospital's see if anyone came in with deep scratches to the face or even an eye gouged. Who knows maybe we'll get lucky? We'll need to get door to door done asap; somebody must have heard something. She would have made a lot of noise when she was getting her fingers cut off." said Marks.

'We need her key and need to find out if anyone else had a key. We need to get onto the company that provides the security to the flats. See if they can tell us who accessed the building, I noticed they have cctv covering the entrance to the flats. Let's see if we can catch him coming in or leaving the flats' said Marks.

There were a few photographs in the bedroom but there didn't seem to be any of deceased with a partner.

They looked around the flat. It was obvious deceased had done well for herself. Everywhere you looked there was designer goods. She was obviously one of those people who thought you get what you pay for.

It appeared as if nothing had been touched in any of the rooms except the bedroom.

Marks entered a small room which the deceased used as her office. Her laptop was there but was off. There didn't appear to be a diary, at least that he could see. Then again, he thought, if deceased had an organiser app on her laptop. 'We'll take that, maybe it'll have a diary of who she was meeting and when' he said to Budd pointing to the laptop.

Marks and Black left the locus and returned to Headquarters where Marks briefed Detective Inspector Thompson on what he had seen regarding the crime scene. Thompson informed Black and Marks of the progress of the enquiry or lack of rather, since they'd left.

Thompson was relatively young in service. He'd only been a Police Officer for nearly 9 years but had risen to the rank of Inspector primarily due to him joining the police on the graduate scheme, where graduates gain accelerated promotion up to Inspector level.

Thompson had achieved this after 7 years but was very good at his job and was tipped by many as a potential Chief Constable.

Although Marks only had 5 years' service left before he retired, he figured by then he'll be calling Thompson sir.

Although Thompson was inexperienced regarding murder enquiries the same could not be said of Marks. He was very experienced in leading the investigation into murder enquiries, having previously being the lead detective, and interview advisor in Dundee's most infamous murders.

The murders of the Callahan family.

The family, husband, wife, two cousins and the cousins' fiancées had been camping in Hampton Park when they were attacked by a knife wielding male. He brutally hacked all 6 to death, decapitating their heads and leaving the heads on different greens of the Hampton golf course. The male responsible was found not guilty by reason of insanity and was sent to a secure mental facility.

Marks got a lot of praise for the way in which he handled the incident. But what people didn't realise was how much this took out of him. Not physically but mentally. He was completely drained at the time and if he was being honest with himself, he had never been the same since. He saw things that no human should ever have to see. Of course, this was years ago when a man was weak if he asked for help, especially with regards to his mental well-being. To this day he couldn't comprehend how anyone could do what that man did that night.

Although he had been involved with murder enquiries prior to this, his faith in human nature evaporated.

What made this especially difficult for Marks was that the male responsible had been a friend of his many years ago. He was on his way to be a star pupil who had the world at his feet. However, he changed, he thought as anybody would, when his brother was shot and killed whilst on duty with the army. The lad idolised his brother. The day his brother died was the day he died, and a killer was born.

CHAPTER 3

Detective Sergeant Jackie Gold had been designated the FLO (Family Liaison Officer) to Elaine Dawson's family. This is a role he fulfilled alongside his everyday duties.

A FLO is the sole point of contact from the police to the victim's family. This enables the police to provide a support network for Elaine's family. Any assistance they required would be provided by the FLO. Whether that may be questions about any part of the investigation or if they had questions surrounding legal issues about the investigation.

They may want assistance from outwith agencies, such as Social Work. They may have specific requests regarding the Autopsy, timescales, procedures, religious beliefs that the police must consider.

From an investigative point of view, it also gives police the opportunity to ask the family questions that may be significant to the enquiry. They may also have questions regarding the legalities of certain aspects of the enquiry especially if the matter went to court.

Gold arrived at Elaine Dawson's parental address. The part of the job that no officer liked, informing family of a loved one's death. Gold knocked at the door, a typical policeman's knock, hammering on the door with his knuckles. After he'd done it, he felt it wasn't necessary, but it was a habit. A frail woman answered.

As soon as she opened the door, she looked at Gold. She knew, call it mother's intuition, but she knew that something had happened to her baby girl.

Photographs of Elaine graduating from university, celebrating milestone birthdays and as a child adorned the living room walls. Gold could see she was a petite, with long jet-black hair, tanned skin, beautiful brown eyes with a slim figure. An only child she appeared to have a happy childhood and she did well at school. She studied hard and had lots of friends at school some of whom she remained in contact with.

When Gold gave them the bad news, they were distraught. The father slumped in his chair; head bowed as he sobbed uncontrollably. The mother said nothing, in shock, hardly able to comprehend what she'd been told.

After a few moments the mother spoke to Gold. She reminisced how Elaine had come home from school without having eaten any of her lunch one day. When her mother asked her why she didn't eat her lunch she said because one of her friends,

Samira, hadn't eaten because it was Ramadan. Elaine not wanting Samira to be left alone, whilst everyone ate their lunch, refused to eat hers, instead opting to play with Samira. This was the kind of girl she was. Elaine's mother was beaming with pride as she told Gold this.

She was always keen to try new things and join new clubs. Between the ages of 6 – 16, she tried her hand at almost everything, playing piano, guitar, tennis, swimming, netball, running, dancing even amateur dramatics.

She never changed when she became an adult. She worked hard and qualified as a lawyer, preferring to concentrate on criminal law. But outside of work she kept fit by going to a gym.

She enjoyed socialising with friends, took up photography a few years ago and was learning Spanish. She was the perfect daughter. Gold could feel the love this mother had for her daughter. Despite working ten to twelve hours a day, most days, she kept in constant contact with her parents, updating them with details of how work was and who she was dating.

Gold got the impression that if they asked to see deceased's room it would be as it was when she left to live on her own. Keeping it as a shrine to their beloved daughter.

Although he knew they weren't going to be able to provide any useful information now, he thought it best to stay for the time being. He had the phone numbers of Victim Support Groups, Social Work, Bereavement groups, and other groups he thought may be able to help them at this time. He always carried this information to give to victim's families.

Back at the station, Operation Rosewater was the name given to the investigation. Marks had no idea how it came to be called Rosewater and he didn't care what it was called if they caught the killer and fast. The incident room was a hive of activity, people going in and out, phones ringing, radio messages being passed.

So far, the police knew very little. Although they were building a bigger picture of deceased's life, by establishing who she was friends with, where she went and with who, but they needed to obtain that nugget of information that would crack the case open.

Marks, like most police officers, thought cctv was a valuable weapon in the fight against crime but was only too aware that as valuable as it can be, 99% of it will be no use. Either the cameras are not zoomed in enough to capture an image or the street lighting is poor. If the cctv operator is lucky enough to catch an incident ongoing then the cctv footage is superb for evidential purposes because you can't deny what people, see you doing. The trouble is there are so many cameras nowadays that the chances of the operator catching a crime as it occurs is slim.

Police learned from deceased's colleagues that she was a sociable and hard-working woman. She was single, through choice and no one knew of any boyfriend in her life. As far as her parents and friends knew she didn't have a date at the weekend.

The results of the scene of crime examination would take a few days but Marks was hopeful DNA would be found and that it would belong to someone with a criminal record. However, he knew, the likelihood of this happening was remote, he couldn't explain it, but he knew this murder enquiry would be a runner. (The name given to an enquiry that will take some time to catch the killer)

Uniformed officers conducted door to door enquiries, but they were met by a host of people who neither knew deceased or didn't see or hear anything.

Marks was hopeful though that the security footage of people entering and exiting the building would enable them to identify the person responsible. After all there was only one entrance and exit. Unfortunately, this was going to take a few days maybe even a week because the hard drive that stores the camera footage is situated in the security companies' HQ in Manchester.

Social media was being checked and dating sites for deceased and any potential suitors.

However, deceased hadn't posted anything on her Facebook account for months and she didn't have twitter account. She did go on a couple of dates with two men she met on a dating app. Although this was three months ago and ten months ago.

These men would have to be traced and at the very least ruled out of the enquiry.

Police didn't find anything of note from deceased's phone and they issued a press release requesting anyone with information to contact police. They also asked the public that any driver or cyclist who had dash-cam footage or go pro footage of the area from over the weekend to hand it in to police.

Unfortunately, at this time they had no idea who they were looking for, what he was wearing or even what deceased was wearing the last time she was seen alive. Nonetheless, Marks thought that if they had the footage secured, they could examine it anytime should they ascertain the movements, and or clothing of deceased or the killer.

Without knowing what deceased was wearing or what the killer was wearing, (Preferably you'd have both) when she was last seen alive and he (assuming the killers male) it would be almost impossible to pick her or him out of the cctv footage. Even if they knew deceased's last movements, they could begin to piece together where she had been, where she was going to and who she met, if anyone.

They knew she'd left work at 5pm on Friday, but did she go straight home in her car? Did she stop off anywhere? Did she meet anyone? Did she change her clothes? Had she arranged for someone to come over? Marks would like the answers to all of these, but the reality was, he'd probably never find out the answers to all these questions. He knew that the review of cctv footage would end up being labour intensive task, but it needed to be done.

Gold contacted Marks. As far as Elaine Dawson's parents were aware there were only three keys to Elaine's flat. Elaine's, which was found on a key rack behind the front door. The second was found in Sharon Edwards' possession and the third they had. So, the killer didn't have a key. Deceased must have allowed him entry to the flat, thought Marks. She must have known him.

A post-mortem was scheduled for 9am tomorrow morning. Both Marks and Thompson would be present for that. Not the most pleasant task, but an essential one, nonetheless.

Marks was exhausted. He was physically and mentally drained. He could feel his body slouching over as if he was carrying the weight of the world on his shoulders. Barely able to keep his eyes open. He needed rest. It was almost 10pm and he decided to leave it for the day. This hadn't been his best day, but it was far from his worst day on the job also. He tried to remain positive but sometimes it was hard given that regardless how hard they worked the crime rate was rising, especially violent crime. He was seeing people commit crime after crime and yet they were receiving lesser sentences in court.

He thought the people who said that it was society's fault people behaved the way they did rather than saying the criminal was to blame give criminals an excuse for their actions. He thought that when you were old enough to understand the difference between right and wrong then you were old enough to take responsibility for your actions.

To top it all he was lonely. He had friends but no one in his life he could share how his day went. No one to enjoy a meal with. No one to ask how their day went and yet almost everyone he knew in the police had someone, even if it was their third wife/husband.
What was wrong with him, he thought. He knew the answer. He'd given his life to the police at the expense of a relationship and a family. He wondered if he were to do it all again would he do the same.

Driving home, he promised himself he was going to make a concerted effort to try and forge a relationship with a woman. This didn't have to be an intimate relationship, just a friend.

Marks hadn't had a partner for some time – all the previous girlfriends realised quite early in the relationship that they were a distant second to the job. He never even went out often. He used to go out for the occasional pint to catch up with some friends or to watch football on tv.

He'd long stopped going to Dundee United games too, besides they were a shadow of the team that won plaudits across Europe for the way they played. The memories of him recalling McAlpine, Hegarty, Narey, Bannon, Milne, Sturrock to name but a few brought a smile to his face. Those were the days.

In a sense he along with others the same age had been spoilt. Whilst United had frequently fell at the final hurdle on the few occasions when they won trophies it was all the sweeter having first suffered the heartache. Especially when he recalled the times United were winning but threw it away. However, he was still proud to say Dundee United were one of the few sides in the world who have beaten Barcelona in every competitive match they've played. Granted they've only played four times, two two-legged games and if they were to play now United would have a hard job keeping Barcelona from scoring ten.

CHAPTER 4

When Marks woke, he could feel his left pinky twitching. He watched it as it twitched rapidly, wondering if he had been lying on a nerve. He got up, went to have a shave and a shower then got dressed in an old suit he had laid out the night before. He didn't wear one of his new suits because experience told him that this suit would need dry cleaned afterwards to get rid of the smell of death.

He attended at the incident room. There were whiteboards full of the names of officers working on the enquiry, their call signs and the shift they were on. This was a task by itself. Not a great deal had happened regarding the murder enquiry throughout the night.

The first 48 hours in a murder enquiry were crucial and yet they had nothing indicating why Elaine Dawson was chosen as the killers' victim. No suspects and they had only narrowed the time of death down by a few hours. Hopefully the post-mortem will provide us with a few clues.
Marks was feeling tired, despite it not even being dinnertime yet. He'd had a long day at work yesterday, and he could still feel the tiredness in his legs. He was finishing delegating today's duties when Black came in to see how things were progressing. He was disappointed with the progress but couldn't fault the effort of the troops.

He wasn't feeling his usual upbeat self, but he couldn't understand why. He had noticed that he had become more negative minded lately. This troubled him because he had always been a positive thinker before.

He was always forgetting things now. This had resulted him making a list of all the things he had to do, at work and at home. The only problem now was remembering where he put the list in the first place.

Dr Dempster was carrying out the post-mortem. She was a relatively small woman in her 50's, very quick witted, and one of the smartest people on the planet thought Marks. A member of Mensa, she enjoyed quizzes. She even had her own team that entered quizzes all around the country, quite often winning. She was also an excellent chess and poker player and had recently won a lot of money in a high stake's poker game. She was one of those people that was naturally very good at, whatever she turned her hand to.

DCI Marks, DI Thompson, DC Martin in his role as SOC (Scenes of Crime) photographer, the Procurator Fiscal were all present as was Dr Dempster's assistant, Tommy. Tommy, appeared to be socially awkward, cracking jokes at the most inappropriate time and not knowing how to act in certain situations. Marks wondered if Tommy was like this before he started working there, or if he became how he is through working there. Either way seemed like the perfect place for somebody like Tommy to work.

All the tools were laid out on a table, scalpel, bone cutters, hand saw, brain knife, cranium chisel, which all conjured up horrifying images. Whilst everything was, as usual, clinically clean.

Marks noticed that the morgue didn't smell as bad as it normally did and remarked upon it to Thompson who said with a screwed-up face 'Is your nose blocked, it's absolutely stinking in here today?' Even for experienced officers the smell of death can sometimes be overwhelming. 17

Dempster's assistant Tommy, filmed the procedure as instructed by the doctor.

Every little thing the pathologist does has to be documented and this process assisted them in doing that. As the saying goes, the camera never lies. Filming the procedure prevented any dubiety regarding deceased's injuries and when they may or may not have occurred.

Dr Dempster took samples of deceased's hair and cuttings of her toenails. These were to be analysed for DNA as they may assist in identifying the killer. She began the post-mortem.
Swabs were taken from the mouth, rectum and deceased's sexual organs.

Dempster revealed that someone had sexual intercourse with deceased after she had died.

There was a good chance they would acquire the killer's DNA because of this.

Dempster then began cutting into the body at the head and neck, as is normal when strangulation is thought to have been the cause of death. She found the hyoid bone had been broken. This confirmed she was strangled. Marks had been to so many of these procedures that he had learnt a great deal watching and listening to the pathologists. The hyoid bone is the only bone in the body not connected to another bone and fractures of the hyoid bone from trauma other than strangulation are extremely rare. This is also the case regarding hangings. The hyoid bone is rarely broken when someone has hung themselves.

There was something in deceased's mouth. Dr Dempster carefully retrieved deceased's underwear from her mouth. This is probably why no one heard any screams. He placed something in her mouth. As far as killers go this one appeared to be calculated. He had thought of potential ways in which his victim could alert others, even after death, by stifling her cries and cutting off her fingers. Dempster confirmed that deceased had a burn like mark on her shoulder and concluded that this could have been as a result of her being struck with a stun gun or tasered.

Marks hated to admit it, but this killer was smart.

The post-mortem was complete. Marks and Thompson returned to the incident room. Marks updated Black about the results of the post-mortem and then phoned the sex offenders unit asking them if they had knowledge of anyone, they were monitoring who had previously had sex with corpses or had cut the fingers off their victims. He was told they would check all the sex offenders they were monitoring but that to their knowledge it no one came to mind.

Marks phoned DS Black. They had been friends for a long time. 'I'm going for some lunch do you want anything?'
'No, I'm fine thanks. Oh, by the way before I forget, Jackie was wondering if you want to come around for dinner on Sunday?' asked Black.
'Sounds great Dave, what time?'

'About four. We can watch whatever games on the tv'
'Great. Thanks Dave. Tell Jackie I'd be delighted to come over'
'Will do.'
That had cheered Marks up a bit. Proper Sunday lunch, football on the telly, superb. Jackie was a nurse, but she was also an excellent cook. Roast tatties, peas, carrots, steak pie. He was salivating at the thought of it.

Whilst he was enjoying his lunch the phone rang. It was Amy Hart, one of the Forensic Scientists at the Forensic Lab. She had analysed the forensic evidence from the Elaine Dawson
 crime scene. She didn't manage to obtain the killers DNA from any of deceased's clothing, but she had identified two different DNA specimens from deceased's body.

However, neither of the specimens had come back as that of anyone whose DNA was already in the national police database. There are roughly 6 million people's DNA on this database. This means that the killer has never been convicted of a crime, or rather never been caught, at least as an adult.

Children who have committed a serious crime such as murder, rape, sodomy, have their DNA removed from the database once they become sixteen.

This was a major blow to Marks and his team. They thought that due to the nature of the murder that the DNA would be someone who was known to them. This means that it could be the first time this killer has struck. The nature of the murder, cutting off fingers, stuffing her throat with something and raping a dying woman was particularly chilling even to the hardened officers on the team.

Detectives had also checked the two people Elaine Dawson had met previously through the dating app, Gordon Harvey and Paul Bell, and it appeared that there was no animosity between her and these men.

Their alibis had been checked by detectives and each of them were ruled out of the enquiry, at least for now.

Enquiries made with the hospital didn't turn up any leads as no one attended Accident and Emergency with a gouged eye or deep scratch marks on the face.

Despite extensive enquiries carried out Marks and his team were nowhere nearer to catching their killer than they were in the first few hours of the investigation.

Dawson's phone had been checked and although there were some texts from Harvey asking Dawson for another date, none of these were explicit or threatening. There were, however, messages to and from a male called Scott. The number they were from was checked through all police systems, but nothing came back in relation to this.

Marks thought this is obviously a bought phone, no contract, so no luck there. If the person who had this phone had it on contract police could easily trace who it belongs to.

The laptop, however, was not going to be examined for weeks due to the backlog the force had.

Although this was a murder enquiry, there were rape enquiries, drug related enquiries and child protection enquiries that were also important and were also reliant upon information stored on these laptops or computers.

They had only managed to narrow the time of death down a little, from nine twenty pm on Friday night when she spoke to a friend about her plans for the summer, to 0930 Monday, when she was discovered about nine thirty am Monday morning by Mrs Edwards. This left police with a gap of 48 hours in deceased's life that they had to account for.

They had established that the murder was most probably sexually motivated, and that the killer got sexual gratification from dominating, controlling and seeing deceased in pain. They thought the killer may have cut off the victims' fingers for his own pleasure.

Fortunately, killers like this are rare. They had been having no luck in their enquiries yet. But their luck was about to change.

Finally, a week after the murder of Elaine Dawson, the cctv footage of the building entrance arrived by courier. Although the concierge was sat in an office locally, the cctv footage had to be copied
 onto a DVD from their security head office in Manchester. It was a bit antiquated but nonetheless, they had it now.

DC Mason was tasked to carry this out. Unfortunately, all police knew about what deceased was wearing the last time she was seen, which was when she left work about 5pm Friday 1st March, was a grey trouser suit. She would have been carrying a briefcase and possibly carrying a black umbrella.

Maybe if he got her on camera entering the building, then he might see if she's alone or had company. Or, if she went out again, what she was wearing. He knew he was in for a long couple of days. He made himself as comfortable as he could then set about trying to find this killer.

CHAPTER 5

It was Christmas morning and the snow had fallen during the night. Outside it was picturesque. The streets were covered in snow. It was a blank canvas. Children everywhere were beginning to wake up. Their faces a picture of excitement, waiting to see what Santa had brought them, before they harassed their parents into getting dressed and dusting off the sledge in the garage.

Mathew was six and all he asked for Christmas was a Star Wars light saber. Mathew loved Star Wars, then again who didn't. Normally a light sleeper, he somehow slept til 8am and had to be woken by his mother.

When he realised what day, it was he sprang up out of bed smiling. You could feel the excitement.
His mother took him over to the window. 'Look outside' she said. He looked out and a look of amazement appeared on his face. His mother was happy. She had gotten used to the frowns and scowls on his face lately that she had forgotten how angelic he looked when he smiled. 'Can we go sledging mum?' he said.
'After we have breakfast and open some presents' came the reply.
Mathew opened some presents, and while he seemed happy with his presents both his mother and father could see a hint of disappointment with each present opened when he realised it wasn't a Star Wars light Saber.

His mother disappeared into the kitchen, reappearing with another present that she had 'apparently forgot'. He knew straight away what is was. The biggest smile appeared on his face as he ripped open the Star Wars Light Saber. 'Thanks mum' as he ran over to her with open arms, giving his mum a hug. A hug. She could hardly believe it. She thought he was becoming more distant with her and his father recently. She didn't know why. Then he ran to his father 'Thanks dad'. 'You're welcome son. Merry Christmas son' said his dad.

He played with it for weeks. His dad had become the enemy. Of course, he only had one light saber, so dad had a finished roll of wrapping paper. Which invariably broke with one swish of the light saber. He then had to use an old stick Mathew had found in the garden.

That was the happiest she had ever seen Mathew; He would never be that happy again.

It was a beautiful summers day, a gentle breeze cooled the kids briefly as they ran, giggled and played at the park. Whilst their parents either fumbled around their bags in desperate search of the sun lotion they would smother the children in or queued in what seemed like a mile-long queue to buy ice lollies, drinks and water to quench their children's thirst.

But there was one child who didn't partake in the joviality the glorious weather had brought.

Mathew, was within his garden, playing with his guinea pigs his father had bought him a few weeks before being killed in a car accident.

He was playing alone not only because he liked his own company but because he'd recently began bullying the other children. Even children that were older than him. All the children seemed to fear him. There was a coldness about Mathew.

His mother, struggling to cope, was indoors, and now in the process of drinking her fifth vodka of the day. She had tried her best but was clearly struggling without Mathew's father.

A few hours had passed before she woke. She immediately went to check on her son Mathew. She found him still in the rear garden, where she had left him. However, she saw a sight that chilled her to the bone. Mathew had killed both guinea pigs. She saw both guinea pigs lying on the grass with their ears cut off, paws cut off and Mathew sitting their humming a tune to himself, his t-shirt covered in blood and most worryingly of all he was smiling.

'Mathew what happened'.
'I got bored playing with them, so I killed them' said Mathew in a very matter of fact way. There was no emotion from Mathew.

She decided there and then she couldn't cope with Mathew's bizarre behaviour and thought it best to send him to his uncle's, if he would take him.

Mathew's mother was hopeful he would get the strict discipline she felt he was requiring. His uncle Terry worked in a slaughterhouse and was the one person Mathew always looked up to. He was tall, strong and not someone to argue with.

That summer was the last she would spend with Mathew. He went to stay with his uncle Terry.

None of their lives would ever be the same again.

Mathew had recently turned twelve years old and by all accounts had a good birthday, spent with Terry, his wife Theresa and their daughter Diane.

But Mathew's behaviour spiralled out of control despite his uncle's best efforts to discipline him. Weeks later he was given up for adoption after Theresa found him masturbating whilst looking at his daughter and her friends playing in the garden. They were only 7 years old at the time.

They no longer wanted anything to do with Mathew.

Heartbroken and alone. Mathews mother drinking got worse until she died a few months later having suffered a heart attack. When she was found she was lying in the foetal position surrounded by empty bottles of wine and vodka.

CHAPTER 6

Friday 15th March and Marks and his team hadn't made much progress regarding Elaine Dawson's murder. Unfortunately for Marks and his team, things were about to go from bad to worse.

Uniformed officers had been called to a house regarding concern for the occupier, a twenty-five-year-old personal trainer, Alison Trent, who hadn't been seen since Wednesday 13th March.

This was apparently totally out of character for her because she hadn't been seen on the Thursday, (Although this was her day off) and she hadn't turned up at the gym for her spin class at 7am.

The attending officers found the door to the house closed. They tried the handle. The door was unlocked. The officers put gloves on and entered. Slowly they opened each door, checking the house for Alison until they found her bound to her bed, naked and minus her fingers on her left hand. The senior officer of the pair immediately contacted the force control room to report what they'd found whilst the younger one ran outside to show the world his breakfast.

Marks was contacted by the control room and informed of their discovery. He couldn't believe what he was hearing. The deceased in this incidence had also had her fingers cut off. She was also in a flat, alone. No way was this a coincidence. He contacted DS Budd and had him attend straight away at locus.

Black had already been made aware and charged into the incident room. He was a seasoned officer who treated everyone with the respect, even probationers who were sometimes looked down upon by senior officers, but he had his 'don't fucking get in my way face on'. As experienced as Marks and Thompson were, they knew not to argue with him.

Although Black wasn't particularly big, he was ex-special forces. Rumour has it, one night when Black was a street sergeant, George Douglas, a notorious hardman from Dundee, pissed him off in the cells. Black had been covering as the custody sergeant for the usual sergeant, who was away to a family function, when Douglas, who had an unrivalled hatred for the police, spat at him, as he checked to see if he was ok. (The sergeant does this every so often in a shift)

No sooner had he spat at him when Black opened the cell door and went in. He came out a few minutes later muttering something under his breath. The custody assistant, not a police officer, stealthily went to check on Douglas and found him bent over clutching his privates. When he saw the custody assistant, he meekly said 'That bastard just kicked me in the nuts, twice!'.

The custody assistant didn't know whether to laugh, after all this was a notorious hardman, or be sympathetic. So, he did what he thought was best and scurried back to his office pretending this hadn't just happened.

Douglas obviously thought against making an official complaint, for obvious reasons. His hardman image would be shattered and everyone would find it hilarious, him being kicked in the nuts, not once but twice.

Marks contacted Budd who had been appointed Crime Scene Manager for this murder too. 'Jimmy any update yet?' asked Marks.

Budd replied 'From what I've seen so far I think it's the same killer as Elaine Dawson's. The scene's the same, nothing appears to have been disturbed or moved in any other rooms other than the bedroom. Clothes strewn about the bedroom floor. Deceased naked, appears to have been strangled, bound by her wrists and ankles to the frame of the bed with cord, which looks like the same stuff he used to tie up Elaine Dawson'.

Budd continued, 'This time however, he cut of her fingers on her left hand. But like the Dawson murder, the fingers aren't here. I'll be finished here in about 30 minutes.
'Ok. I'll contact Dr Dempster and DS Black and I will meet the doctor at locus. See you in about 30 minutes' said Marks.

Marks left Thompson in charge at the incident room, he was the deputy SIO after all, and attended at the house where the latest victim had been discovered accompanied by DS Black.

Marks, Black and Dr Dempster arrived simultaneously at the locus. Budd who had already been there for some time came out to meet them.

The house was among the first of three houses set back from the main road. Large hedges surrounded the properties and therefore it was unlikely anyone would have seen anyone at the house, apart from the someone at the other two properties. He could see that as he got closer to the front door, anyone within the flat could see, if the curtains were open, someone approaching the house from the living room window.

The driveway to deceased's house was loose stones, so maybe someone heard something thought Marks. There was no cctv anywhere close to the locus.

Pleasantries exchanged Marks, Black and Dempster put on Forensic suits which included forensic paper shoes. They were like the ones you get at the swimming that you cover your shoes with. They had to ensure they did not contaminate the crime scene in any way. Once they were already, they entered the locus. Marks noted that once again, there was no forced entry.

He couldn't see any blood anywhere in the hall, albeit the walls of the hall were dark red. He thought it gave the hall a very regal look. Gold framed mirror at the end of the hall and gold framed photographs including what appeared to be a portrait of deceased. He could have been forgiven if he thought he was in a stately home.

When he entered the living room, there was a slimline TV, which wasn't particularly big, which he thought was slightly unusual these days, and a host of workout dvds lying next to the tv stand. Oak wooden flooring, a beige rug, cream two-seater sofa, two armchairs and a nest of tables, one of which had a cream coloured vase on with fresh lillies inside. It was all very neat and cosy.

They walked into the bedroom and saw clothes lying on the floor. Jogging bottoms, t-shirt, sports bra but no underwear. Marks wondered if the killer had taken these or like the first victim, had them stuffed in her throat.

Sure enough, Dr Dempster saw there was something stuffed into her throat, but she couldn't retrieve the item, but like Marks she believed this item would be found to be her underwear. The clothing would later be taken for forensic examination.

Marks was wondering if there was any significance in why the fingers on her left hand were missing.
Why the right hand of Elaine Dawson's? Was Alison Trent left-handed, was Elaine Dawson right-handed? If they were, then how did the killer know this, and what is the significance of cutting their fingers off their dominant hand?

Dr Dempster was examining the body. 'One more and you've got yourself a serial killer gentleman' she said.

Marks, Black and Budd never said anything, choosing to stay quiet but all fearing the worst. They knew she was right. A serial killer in Dundee. Never. That only happens in big cities like London, New York and Moscow not Dundee.

Although a serial killer, by definition, is someone who commits at least 3 murders over more than a month with an emotional cooling off period, (this could be days, weeks, months or even years).

Are they, the public, going to argue that these murders aren't the work of a serial killer I highly doubt there were far too many similarities between them both?

Although Britain has had its share of serial killers throughout the years, fortunately they are very rare. Unfortunately, however when you think of serial killers your brain automatically thinks of American serial killers such as Ted Bundy, Jeffrey Dahmer, John Wayne Gacy, Richard Ramirez and Albert De Salvo. This could be because when you think of these killers you recall that not only did, they kill their victims, some of them ate their victims, had sex with their corpses and showed absolutely no remorse for their crimes. Some, revelling in their notoriety.

'Bloody hell' said Marks, 'the press will have a field day with this'.

The doctor carried out her examination of deceased as best she could and concluded that like the first victim, Elaine Dawson, this victim had been alive when her fingers had been cut off. She appeared to have been strangled and raped after death. Also, like the first victim she had a small burn mark, but this was on the nape of her neck.

Marks thanked the doctor for her attendance and said he'll be in touch to arrange the post-mortem. Marks and Black inspected deceased's house for any evidence items had been moved or stolen but nothing appeared to have been disturbed.

'Jimmy give us a shout if you get anything. We're going back to the incident room' said Marks. 'Ok, boss' he replied.

They knocked at the doors of the adjoining houses, but it looked like the house on the end was in the process of being renovated. The house in the middle of the three had curtains that looked as if they belonged in the 1930's. They got no reply from this house. They would need to have uniform officers re-attend later.

CHAPTER 7

Black had been summoned to Chief Constable Harkins' office. They discussed Marks' ability to continue as SIO in the murder investigations. Unknown to Marks his senior officers had noticed the changes in his health, and they were worried about him, as well as his ability to lead a murder investigation. Black's loyalty was never in doubt. He said that there was no question, as to whether Marks was the best person to lead the investigation. Whilst the Chief Constable appreciated where his loyalties lay, she made it clear that if she thought his ability to handle the investigation was compromised in any way, she would replace him as Senior Investigating Officer.

Meanwhile, Marks had only been in the incident room a matter of seconds when Detective Constable Mason entered.

It had been exactly 2 weeks since the first murder victim, Elaine Dawson had been found and DCI Marks was about to get a nasty shock.

Mason entered the incident room, 'Sir. I've been reviewing the footage from Elaine Dawson's building'.
'And? Anything of interest on it?' said Marks.
'Can I speak to you in your office' he whispered.

Marks could tell that whatever it was wasn't good.
'Sure'
When they got into Marks' office, Marks said, 'I take it you've something you didn't want to share with the rest of the team to tell me?'
'Yes' came the reply. 'I've looked through the security footage of deceased's building, at least some of it, and I found deceased enter at 1742:32. She enters and walks to the lift. Gets in the lift and then she's lost to sight'.
She doesn't leave the building after that.

However, at 23:15:25 it appears as if police attended at a flat in the building on Friday night. The male enters, goes up the stairs and is lost to sight'.

'What. No one thought to tell us this' said Marks.
'Well, that's the problem sir. I've checked with the control room and police didn't receive a call to the building on Friday night. In fact, police haven't received a call to attend any flat in the building for over a year!'.
'Ah for fuck sake....can you identify who the cop is?'
'No, he keeps his head down, doesn't look up at the camera, and you can't identify his shoulder number from the camera, because you would need to zoom in on that'.
'What about when he leaves?' said Marks.
'No, he comes down the stairs and leaves pretty quickly' replied Mason.
'How long was he in the building for?'

'He left at 23:55;17 sir, so about 40 minutes'
'That doesn't seem like enough time to commit this crime' replied Marks.

'So, we either have someone pretending to be a cop, probably to gain access to the flats. Or a police officer could be responsible for this? Either way it's not good'.

They were all too aware what this could mean.

'Right. You continue finishing the cctv review. Report only to me. I'll let John (DI Thompson) know what you've found, and I'll need to let the DS Black know. Under no circumstances does anybody else know' barked Marks.
'Yes sir' said Mason.
'Oh and let me know if you find anything else of interest on the footage' shouted Marks.

Mason said 'ok' and gave him the thumbs up.

Marks immediately went along to DS Black's office and informed him of the development.

Black informed the Chief Constable. They agreed they would try to ascertain whether it was a real police officer before they went public with this. However, they would need to try and do this ASAP, otherwise the public would think the police are trying to cover it up. How would the public ever trust the police again if this was the case?

They decided they would carry out a GPS signal check on all officers' radios. This would indicate if an officer's radio was in the vicinity of deceased's home over the weekend the murder occurred.

This could be done quickly, quietly and without people's knowledge. However, they were aware that this could only pinpoint the radio to roughly 25/30 metres, but it would give them a place to start.

Black knew there was no reason for any officer to be in the vicinity of Elaine Dawson's flat.

The GPS signal result came back. PC Scott Young, a beat officer with 4 years' service. The name didn't ring any bells with him. However, that wasn't necessarily a bad thing, because it meant his name hadn't been brought to his attention for something untoward.

He checked the duty sheets on his computer. Young was on duty now. Marks contacted him and asked him to come down to Headquarters, to assist CID with enquiries relating to the murders.

Marks and Thompson were notified by the custody sergeant that Scott Young was downstairs looking for them. They wanted to get him into a room as fast as possible to reduce the chances of officers quizzing him about why he was there.

Marks and Thompson left what they were doing and went straight down to the PEO (Public Enquiry Office)
'Scott, Hi I'm DCI Conor Marks and this is DI John Thompson, can we have a chat?'.
They all knew that Marks' question was a rhetorical one.
'Yeah sure, what's this about? replied Young.
'We'll tell you when we get upstairs, nothing to worry about just some queries about your shift last Friday' said DCI Marks.
'This will do' said Marks as he opened the door to an empty interview room.

'Sit there,' said Thompson, pulling out a seat for Young.
'Thanks' came the reply.
'Now, we'll get you to sign these voluntary attendance forms. We'll caution you but you're free to go anytime you like' said Marks.
Young although relatively inexperienced knew this. 'ok'.

Marks began to ask him questions.

'Who were you paired up with on Friday?' asked Marks
'Sarah Stewart' said Young.
'Were you together all night or did you go to any calls on your own?'
'We were together all night'
'Was last Friday a busy shift?'
'Yeah, why?'
'Do you recall getting a call to Kings Avenue?'
'No'.
Thompson and Marks were looking at Young closely for any tell-tale signs he was lying. But Young never broke eye contact.
'Were you at any call near to Kings Avenue on Friday night?'
'No, we were nowhere near there on Friday. What is this about?' said Young
'Did you have your own radio on Friday, or did you need to use a pool radio?'
'I had my own radio. Why? I think you should either let me go, or I think I'll need to speak to a solicitor' said Young.
'Ok' said Marks. 'But just a couple of more questions. You had your own radio. Were paired up with Sarah Stewart all night and were never in Kings Avenue. Is that right?
'Yeah that's right' said Young.
'You are aware that a person was murdered last Friday at a flat in Kings Avenue?'
'Yes'
'Do you want to reconsider what you told us previously about not being in Kings Avenue, because according to the GPS signal on your radio you were in Kings Avenue between 2315 hours and 2355?

Marks and Thompson could see Young shift in his seat. Feeling he was needing a little prompting, Marks said 'C'mon son whatever you were doing there, now's your chance to say, this is a murder enquiry after all, and I'm sure whatever you've done, we can sort it'.

'OK' said Young head in his hands now. They could see him muttering something under his breath. 'Ok', I was having an affair with Elaine Dawson. We'd met up on a night out a few months ago. One thing led to another and we ended up at hers.'
'How long has this been going on for?' asked Marks.
'A few months' came the reply. 'My wife will fucking kill me!'
'Maybe son but that's your problem. Did you see Elaine on the Friday night?' said a very unsympathetic Marks.
'Yes.' said Young
'And?'
'And we had sex, but that's all, when I left, she was alive' said Young worryingly.
'How did you think you were going to get away without letting us know this after all your DNA is going to be at the scene' Marks stated.
'I don't know'
'Have you got proof that you were in a relationship with Elaine Dawson?'
'I have text messages from her' said a now sobbing Young.
'Let us see them'
'They're on my other phone in my locker'
'Ok, then we'll go and get it'
Marks and Thompson got Young's locker keys from him and whilst Marks and Thompson stayed with him, Marks asked DS Laws to go and retrieve the phone form Young's locker which was the station he worked from.

Whilst Laws was away to retrieve the phone Marks and Thompson reminded Young that he was still on a voluntary attendance and that he can leave anytime her wanted.

They didn't however tell him that as a result of what he had told them, he would be detained for the murder of Elaine Dawson.

He said she was still alive when he had left her, but he could be lying. Marks and Thompson didn't think, judging by his body language, that he was responsible for the murder, but they weren't going to take a chance and let him go until they were one hundred percent sure he wasn't.

DS Laws returned a short time later and gave the phone to Marks. Marks asked Young to unlock the phone which he did.

'Are the messages under her name?' asked Marks
'Yeah. I bought the phone for her to contact me so if my wife looked on my phone, she would be none the wiser. There's only messages from her on it' said Young.

Marks began looking through the messages. Sure, enough there were numerous messages to and from Elaine Dawson's mobile phone. They were all about the affair.

Crucially the last one was sent to Young's phone was around five past midnight on Saturday 2nd March when she had text him saying that she wished he could stay the night.

He hadn't replied to that message. Marks showed Thompson the messages. They concluded that the only thing Young appeared guilty of was bad judgement, something everyone had been guilty of at one time or another. It also meant they could narrow the time down by a few hours in which deceased was killed.

Marks then said to Young that he would be treated as a witness at this time but that may change depending upon how the investigation goes.

Young gave a statement and signed the phone over to police. He was informed that they couldn't speculate on how this would affect his job but for the time being he was suspended.

Young nodded his head, resigned to the fact that not only had he jeopardised his career but also his marriage. He broke down again. His marriage would be over. What an idiot.

Marks also informed him that his DNA would be compared to that of DNA found in the body of deceased.

CHAPTER 8

Saturday March 16th. It was early afternoon and Marks was beginning to feel the pace of the day. He needed to sit, and not for two minutes. He needed twenty, thirty minutes he felt.

Marks was noticing that no two days were the same. One day he would in a very positive frame of mind, be full of energy, have a bit of banter with the detectives and be focused at work.

But there would also be days where despite sleeping for ten hours, having a healthy breakfast be dressed and ready to go to work but just feel flat. Little energy, no motivation and had a couldn't care less attitude – to everything.

When he felt like that, he didn't want to be around anyone, speak to anyone or do anything, he simply wanted to be alone. Not because anyone had said or done anything to annoy or anger him, in fact it was often quite the opposite.

People generally noticed when he was 'in a mood' and would make even more of an effort to be understanding and go out of their way to help him, but, and he had trouble understanding this himself, he just wanted to be left alone.

This however made him quite unpredictable in every way. Even when things were going his way, he'd be shouting and losing his temper with people, then when he thought about it later, he would be riddled with guilt. It was the unpredictability of it all which bugged him the most. After all he'd risen to the rank of Chief Inspector, a role you would never get to if you weren't seen as being reliable. His small batch of loyal friends would also say he was the most honest and reliable person in the world. He was starting to question himself though.

He was also less confident and decisive in every aspect of his life and this had a ripple effect on him because it increased his anxiety and slowed his movements down even further. This made him more tired physically as well as psychologically.

He was starting to think it was something more than Carpal Tunnel Syndrome, but he had no idea what.

At that point DC Mason knocked on his door. By this time Marks had returned to his office for a welcome sit down. 'Come in' said Marks.

'Sir, I've finished the cctv review of Elaine Dawson's building. Unfortunately, because of the bad weather I couldn't identify quite a few people. However, I went over the statements of people who lived in the building, checked when they said they returned home and what they said they were wearing. Once I did that, I managed to get all but a 2 people identified.' stated Mason.

They're not great because of the weather the people coming and going had hoods up and hats on. Although we do get a good facial image of one of the people, the second person has a hat on but appears to be carrying a bag.

'That's a start Sam. That's great, get photos of the two of them on Can U Id? We'll maybe even release them to the press if we have no joy' said Marks.

'Can U id? is a page on the police intranet which covers all forces in Scotland, although England, Northern Ireland and Wales have ones also. Images are place on this in the hope that an officer somewhere will identify the person.

Marks sat for a further ten minutes until his legs no longer felt like jelly before going to the incident room where he and Thompson tried to establish a link between the two victims whose names had been written on a whiteboard.

1st. Elaine Dawson, b. 14/02/77, single, lawyer – 64 Kings Ave, Dundee, 5ft 6, slim, short black hair, 2nd. Alison Trent, b. 04/04/93, single, personal trainer – 41 Barnes Rd, Dundee, 5ft 5, slim, long blonde hair

Both lived alone. Both were single.

Marks knew they would also have to put a great deal of thought into this next press release because they couldn't deny there were similarities between the two murders.

The post-mortem was arranged for later today, 2pm Saturday 16th March.

DC Paula Crighton had been assigned as the Family Liaison Officer for the Trent family. She would be the link between the investigation and the victim's family.

Black, Marks and Thompson discussed what could possibly link the two victims. The list was endless they thought but decided to concentrate on past boyfriends, places they frequented, web sites they shared, friends and work colleagues. They remained hopeful a link could be found because they knew most murder victims knew their killers. Very rarely is someone murdered by a stranger.

ALISON TRENT

Crighton had learned that Alison Trent was the younger of two sisters. Her sister Cheryl was her best friend and they confided in one another. Alison had always been interested in keeping fit, therefore it was only natural that she became a personal trainer, something that she loved doing. Even in her spare time she kept fit and had been attending Krav Maga classes for about a year.

Crighton had heard of Krav Maga but didn't know anything about it.

She lived alone but had recently started dating a bank manager who frequented the gym called Kevin Ferguson. Although her parents hadn't met him Alison had mentioned him a few times to her sister, Cheryl. She was quite excited by this because Kevin and she appeared to have the same outlook on life, albeit, she thought he was a bit too concerned with having the latest designer clothes, watches and gadgets. Alison wasn't materialistic at all; in fact, she was happiest when she was dressed in her trackies spending time with family and friends. She would rather be skint and be happy than have a career doing something her heart wasn't in.

Alison was an outgoing, positive person who brought out the best in people. She didn't have any enemies, in fact, you would be hard pressed to name a person that didn't like Alison.

Before Crighton finished talking to Cheryl she obtained Kevin's details in order that she trace and speak with him. Crighton contacted him on his mobile and he agreed to meet tomorrow (Tuesday 19th March) afternoon.

Whilst she had time to kill before meeting Kevin Ferguson, she decided to research what Krav Maga was. A martial art created by a Hungarion-Israeli man called Ima Lichtenfeld for the Israeli Army and Special Forces. It was derived from him from a variety of sources including karate, wrestling, boxing, aikido, judo and emphasises aggression and realistic fighting techniques. The emphasis is also on simple techniques that can be used repeatedly in fighting situations.

When they train, they frequently wait until the students are exhausted before they practice any martial arts moves. The theory behind this is that unlike other martial arts where you practice the moves whilst you have energy, they work on the premise that if you can defend yourself when you are exhausted and your adrenaline is pumping you can do it anytime.

Krav Maga also targets the 'soft' areas of the body, such as genitals, eyes, throat, neck, knees etc. Sounds brutal she thought.

Once again Marks, Thompson, DS Budd and DC Martin was there. The Procurator Fiscal and Dr Dempster were also present as was the doctor's assistant, Tommy.

'Good morning all' the doctor said with a saddened tone to her voice. 'Morning doctor' said Marks 'Morning' said Thompson and the Procurator Fiscal.

Tommy had already set the table so to speak, Brain Knife, Cranium Chisel etc etc.

Marks thought they all sounded like bad rock group names but said nothing. He was all too aware the sombre mood in the room. As happy as the doctor normally was, the current situation of her having to perform a post-mortem on a second murder victim in a month dampened everyone's mood.

'The time is 2pm on Saturday 16th March, deceased is Alison Trent, born 4th April 1993' said Dr Dempster as Tommy began filming the procedure.

For Marks and Thompson, it was almost a repeat of the post-mortem of Elaine Dawson's. Cause of death – manual strangulation. Fingers cut off prior to death and once again the victim had been raped after death. Hopefully this will mean more DNA recovered. The doctor did however find another injury on deceased. She had a burn like mark on the back of her neck.

Also, like Elaine Dawson, she had scarring at the back of her throat, meaning something had been forced in her throat prior to her death. The killer had removed this item.

'That marks a burn mark, like from a stun gun or a taser. Elaine Dawson had the same mark on the left shoulder' said Thompson. The burn mark was two little holes roughly an inch apart. Thompson remarked that it looked like a snake bite.

Marks said 'maybe that's how he manages to control his victims. He incapacitates her with an electric shock and then does what he wants to her. By the time she comes around he's got her tied to the bed'.

'But if it's on the back of her neck, she must've trusted him, I mean you wouldn't turn your back on someone you didn't feel safe, around would you?' said Thompson.

'She must have known him, at least well enough to let him into the flat' said Marks.

They finished the post-mortem which had taken up most of the morning while Marks had the unenviable task of issuing a statement to the Press in the afternoon.

Marks made his way back to his office, whilst Thompson offered to go and get him a sandwich for his dinner. Thompson returned with a large portion of stovies for Marks and a coffee, Great thought Marks, he hadn't had stovies for years. He'd forgotten how much he'd liked them. Of course, they weren't as good as the ones his mum used to make, but then again, no Scottish person ever admitted someone made better stovies than them. It was like an unwritten law.

He ate the lot. Not only that but it was the first time in a long time he could remember getting left to eat his dinner without someone somewhere phoning him about an enquiry.

CHAPTER 9

Marks, although experienced in investigating serious crimes, had only given a couple of press releases in his career. He never had and was never likely to seek the limelight. He knew behind the face of a seemingly brilliant detective, as portrayed by the media, there's a large team of police officers. He always likened a police investigation to an American football game.

You may have your starting team, (like beat officers who note the initial complaints) but when you need it, you can bring special teams into play. (like detectives, Forensic, Road Traffic, Fraud, Drugs branch etc)

When he entered the room where the press was situated, he could see numerous journalists with their dicta-phones at the ready, poised like cobras, ready to ask a whole host of questions.

Cameramen stood waiting on the starters pistol, whilst Marks stood, looking the picture of calmness, whilst inside he was extremely nervous.

He began by greeting all who had attended and thanked them for their attendance.

He then wished to, on behalf of Tayside Police, express his sorrow and offer his sympathy to both families at this time. He stated that police were aware that the Dundee public appeared to have decided that both murders were linked. He said that although both murders shared similarities, police had set up two teams to investigate these murders separately. He further stated that Dundee was still a safe place to live and he urged people to continue living their lives as they did before but to be vigilant.

He said police were increasing officers on the street and he urged anyone with information, however small, that they believe may be of use to police then please feel free to contact any officer or attend any police station. He also passed the non- emergency number. It never ceased to amaze him how many people didn't know this. In his experience people thought you phoned 999 for anything to do with the police, even if it was to report a lost dog.

As soon as he had finished talking the gang of journalists began firing questions at him. He expected this but as he stated in his reply to the first, second, third and fourth question he couldn't comment on various aspects of the murders due to the being investigations ongoing.

This would only lead to speculation by the newspapers about the two murders being linked. Marks was aware of this, but he couldn't for obvious reasons divulge at deal of information.

The journalists' questions dried up when they realised, they weren't going to goad him into providing more information about the murders. Again, he thanked them for coming and ended the press conference.

CHAPTER 10

Kevin Ferguson was to attend Police Headquarters at 2pm. Bang on time he appeared. He attended on his own, no solicitor in sight. Not that he needed one after all he was only there to give a statement.

Paula Crighton went to speak with him. She immediately saw that he was very attractive. He was tall, athletic, had a well-kept beard, had short black hair and had tattoos on both forearms. She didn't realise it was his day off and she was glad it was because his muscles made the Armani t-shirt, he was wearing look two sizes too small for him. A well-dressed man who looked good, had brains, brawn and judging by his designer clothes and the Omega Seamaster watch he was wearing had money. Ticked all the right boxes for her.

Crighton thought he came across as being very confident, articulate and honest. She discovered he was a bank manager for the Royal Bank of Scotland. A non-smoker who liked to keep fit he also liked his designer clothes, drove a Mercedes and lived in a flat at Discovery Quay.

He said he met Alison a months ago at the gym but that they had only been on a few dates, but he thought it was too early to say if there was a future together. They spent one night together the previous weekend at her house (weekend 9th, 10th March).

The last time he spoke to her was on Thursday 14th March around 7pm. She said she was staying in because she was early for a spin class at 7am on the Friday. I said I'd phone her Friday night and we can think about doing something over the weekend. She seemed happy at that.

Crighton thanked him for coming in and thought he appeared to be genuine. He seemed to be in disbelief that someone could do this to Alison. She also thought that he raised a good point when he said whoever killed her must have drugged her or incapacitated her in some way.

He thought this because although he'd only known her on a personal level for a few weeks, he recalled 'toy fighting' with her and she caught him on the face with a punch he never saw coming.
Crighton then proceeded up the stairs, with his statement in hand and went to the incident room.

Marks wasn't there so she went to his room. The door was closed. Strange she thought he normally has it open for anyone to pop in for advice or guidance.

She knocked on the door, 'come in' said Marks. He had retreated to his office to try and get some lunch without being interrupted. Guess that planned failed he thought. 'Sorry sir you got a minute' she said.

'Always got a minute for you Paula' said Marks.

'I just took a statement from Kevin Ferguson, Alison Trent's current partner, albeit they've only had a few dates, but I thought he was very genuine.

He last saw her Sunday morning, after staying the night. He says he left about 10am. He last heard from her about 7pm on Thursday 14th March. But he said something very interesting.

He said Alison had been practising a martial art called Krav Maga for about a year and that she was very good at it. If that was the case how did the killer manage to get her under control and tied to the bed, because it sounds like she would've put up a helluva fight'.

Marks replied 'good point Paula, and good work. The doctor did find a burn like mark on the back of her neck'.
'So it must have been someone she trusted for her to turn her back on him' said Crighton.
'That's what John and I thought. Even then he must be strong to carry her to the bedroom, unless of course she took him in there' stated Marks. 'You sure about the new boyfriend?'
'Yeah, but I'll do all the background checks on him anyway of course' 'Good let me know how you get on' 'ok sir' said Crighton as she left to return to the incident room.
Marks gave her the thumbs up as he returned to eat what was left of his lunch.

Marks thought this would then mean Alison was killed between 7pm Thursday and ten past 8 on Friday.

Marks received a call from Amy at the Forensic lab. The swabs taken from deceased Alison Trent's body had come back. Although DNA was found on deceased it wasn't linked to anyone on the national database.

DC Mason received an email from PC White. He identified one of the males in the images he had put on the Can U Id board. The male was Neil Purvis one of the concierges at deceased's building.
Mason put his name through all police computer systems. He was known to police as an offender having committed an assault a few years ago whilst on a night out. According to the report he stated his occupation was a martial arts instructor. But according to their records his DNA was not on file.

Mason informed the DCI.

The DCI was a bit puzzled as to why a concierge would be in the building after midnight. Surely if you can see anyone entering and leaving from the comfort of a warm office why go out especially in such horrible weather. Mason was instructed to go to the concierge office and ascertain what time and date he was next working. He was also asked to get his home address and contact phone numbers in case they couldn't reach him at work.

Mason attended there with PC Kelly who had been seconded to CID for 3 months recently to assist in the murder enquiries. He was quite quiet and was not the usual character you would see in CID, a bit flash, sharp suits, designer specs, walking with a swagger and a bit of a know it all. He knew his stuff when it came to the law though, then again, he did graduate from university with a law degree.

They arrived at the concierge office and spoke with the concierge supervisor. He advised them that Neil was on holiday for a week. Apparently, he was visiting family in England.

He wasn't due back until Sunday 24th March when he started at 3 o'clock and finished at 11pm.

Mason obtained his home address and contact numbers, only after reminding the supervisor that it was a murder investigation they were dealing with. He had tried to quote the Data Protection Act as his defence for not providing any information for Purvis. However when asked which regulation he was referring to the caved and gave the information.

CHAPTER 11

Marks had spoken to Dave (Detective Superintendent Black) and arranged time off for the appointment. He was feeling very nervous. He thought about what his doctor had told him, but he had a feeling it was something more sinister.

He arrived at the hospital and found the waiting area easily enough. He had only been waiting about 2/3 minutes when the doctor appeared.

'Conor Marks' she asked.

'Yes' he replied.

'Hi. Come this way'

'Thanks'

'Have a seat'

'Thanks'

'How are you feeling today?' she said.

'A bit tired but ok'

'Now I'm going to ask you a strange question, but I want you to be honest with me'

'Ok'

'Do you have a sense of smell?'

'No'

'Right. Well as you know you've undergone numerous tests and scans and I have the results of these.'

'Ok'

'What we were looking for, based on the symptoms you had was either a Brain Tumour, MS or to see if you've had a stroke'

Marks looked at the doctor and never said a word. But he was thinking, *Bloody hell, just as well you never told me that, a Brain Tumour, MS, Stroke....*

'Fortunately your test results showed it was none of these. Unfortunately however, you have Parkinson's Disease'

What the Fuck? He thought. 'Parkinson's Disease. Isn't that something you get when you're old and when you shake all the time? I'm only 45' said an astonished Marks.

'Unfortunately, it can happen to young people as well. There are many different ailments to Parkinson's. Tremors is only one part of it. You don't have the tremors. You are slow and steady. So your movements will become slower'.

The doctor quite clearly saw Marks was in shock. To try and provide some comfort she said 'You don't die because of Parkinson's; people die with it. It will affect your quality of life but to what extent we don't know because Parkinson's is such an individual disease. So what affects you might not affect someone else and vice versa.'

'So what is Parkinson's?' asked Marks 'Parkinson's is caused by a lack of a chemical in the brain called dopamine' Marks tried to listen but was lost. He was aware the doctor was speaking but he hadn't heard a single word after dopamine. Marks couldn't even remember what happened after that he recalled sitting in his car staring into space, wondering how will this affect him, at work, at home, with his friends? Everything had just gone from being important to irrelevant.

He drove home. He didn't return to work that week. He didn't inform them about his diagnosis. He still needed time to digest it himself.

As hard as he tried, he could remember one thing and that was that according to the doctor, experts reckon that by the time you're diagnosed you've probably had it for about 7-10 years.

Even when his phone rung, he noticed it was Dave Black, the Detective Superintendent, who was a good friend, he didn't answer. He wasn't in the mood for anyone, regardless if they were a good friend or not, he needed to be left alone.

0530 hours, Monday Marks' alarm clock rang. He jumped up. He'd been in a deep sleep. His first thought was Parkinson's, how will it affect me today? He couldn't help it. Ever since his diagnosis on it was all he could think about.

Dave Black came in to see him almost as soon as he heard a door in the corridor being opened.
Marks informed him about his diagnosis. He was gutted, they were good mates. Whatever you need. Time off, change of hours, work from home, whatever you need we'll do it.

'Thanks' said Marks. He couldn't help himself the diagnosis was all he thought about. He hadn't thought of it before, but how was this going to affect him at work?

For the 1st time since his diagnosis his thoughts switched from the murder investigation to his mother. Her health had deteriorated rapidly in the last few months, after she had fallen in her home.

Unfortunately because he was working and his brother now lived in Southampton, she lay on the kitchen floor for several hours before staff from meals on wheels, (a service he had somehow managed to persuade her to use) discovered her lying confused, and in pain.

Of course he went to her aid immediately, leaving in the middle of yet another meeting, not that anyone made an issue of this.

Fortunately she hadn't broken anything, but she was becoming more and more unsteady on her feet.

This caused him to call his brother Kevin, who was insisting she move down to sheltered accommodation down near him. This really pissed him off. His mother was lucky if she received a call from Kevin once a month since he moved down South 12 years ago. So what changed? He knew the answer that question. His mother had a relatively big house, at least for a pensioner living on her own. The mortgage on the house had been paid for a long time, so once it was sold the money would be split between him and Kevin.

The only reason Kevin wanted mum down there now was so that he can get her to give him Power of Attorney over her money. But he wasn't even sure if the person with the Power of Attorney could do that. He was going to have research this. His understanding was that the Attorney would control the persons finances and if he was right it would allow his brother to take money out of her account whenever "she" needed it, which if he knew his brother would be at least once a week.

That's not happening he thought. For a few moments' exhaustion wasn't the only emotion running through his body. He was angry. He fumbled around his pocket for his house keys. He found them, opened the door and went to the living room. He just sat in his chair for what seemed like a split second and woke up, freezing, hours later. He went to bed. He couldn't sleep so he thought to himself that he might as well go and make himself useful and he researched Power of Attorney. He had no idea it was so complex. From what he understood, it appeared that there are several options regarding the POA (Power of Attorney).

It depended on whether the person could look after themselves physically and mentally. Were they capable of looking after their finances? Could they do it all for themselves, or only do some of it? The person with POA could control all their finances, or part of it and this could be for a period (Like if someone went into hospital but were expected to make a full recovery. Or they may only be granted permission, as the Attorney, to pay bills)

Marks' head was burst, and he decided he would speak to solicitors provided by the Police Federation to see if they could tell him the best way to deal with this.

He believed his mother, whilst there was no doubt, she was getting more forgetful, she was still compus mentus regarding her finances, but for how long. It wasn't that he wanted to control her finances, he simply wanted her to make an informed decision, after all she was a very clever woman. But he had decided to leave it to the professionals.

CHAPTER 12

Black informed the Chief Constable about Marks' diagnosis.

'Sorry Dave, I know your good friends and Conor is vastly experienced, but we'll need to take him off the case'

'Is there any way we can keep him on it, at least to see how he is getting on? I'll monitor him closely, and if there's the slightest doubt he's no longer capable of carrying out the enquiry, then we take him off the case. I mean, I don't know how it'll affect him in the next few months, do you?'

'No I don't. But can we take that chance?'

'The man's devoted his entire adult life to the police, I think we owe it to him to give him the benefit of the doubt. Like I said the first sign that he's struggling or making mistakes, we take him off the case'

The Chief Constable was sceptical about this, but she had faith in Black.

'OK. But keep me updated, daily'

'No problem'

Black was on his way out of Headquarters when he almost bumped into DCI Marks.

'Is that you just finishing Conor?' asked DS Black.

'Yes. It's been another long day' replied Marks

'Fancy a quick pint?'

'Yeah why not. O'Neill's?'

'Sounds good' said the DS.

They both put the briefcases in their cars and walked round to O'Neill's.

O'Neill's was about 100 yards from Headquarters. A traditional Irish pub with its stone flooring, a shillelagh on the wall, traditional Irish music, friendly atmosphere and plenty of Guinness served by either young big bearded Irishman or the wee Irish lassie, dressed all in black with her hair tied back.

A lot of cops drank here for several reasons not just because it was the nearest one to Headquarters.

Another reason was its clientele were older than most of the establishments in the city centre. There was rarely a young wannabe gangster in the place looking to gain a reputation. It was full of mature folk wanting to enjoy themselves and have a good craic.

Also, because it was a loud place, with music and people having a laugh, cops could talk shop, if they wanted without fear of being overheard.

Dave and Marks both nodded to the doormen both of whom said 'Arite fellas' in thick Irish accents.

You could hear the music blasting out as soon as the doors opened. A live band was on. Marks thought they sounded quite good although he had no idea what they were singing, he gave up listening to music when Guns n' Roses split up. Everyone in the place seemed to be enjoying themselves.

Dave ordered them a pint of Guinness each, after all, you couldn't order anything else in an Irish pub.

Typically on a Friday night the place was swarming with cops, all partying hard, after having a tough week. Dave and Marks acknowledged them with a raise of their glass. They sat in the only seats available. They were beside a party of women out for a hen party.

In between screams of excitement and raucous laughter they spoke about their time in the job, after all, Conor had nothing else to speak about. He'd been single for a while, not surprisingly, as all he did was work. Dave had a successful marriage. He'd been married to his childhood sweetheart Jackie for 28 years, they had two sons and two daughters along with a successful career in the police whilst Jackie was a doctor. Marks often wondered how they managed the hours they worked along with bringing up 4 great kids.

David was a marine, Scott was a policeman (Sgt with the Scottish Crime Squad), Katie was training to be a midwife and Bethany was in Advertising.

Conor and Dave had been mates for years. One pint quickly became 4, by which time they had drunk too much to drive. Dave noticed Conor's speech was becoming a bit slurred. He thought it had been a while since they shared a few beers, but he never usually got this drunk on just 4 pints.

He phoned Jackie, his wife, to pick them up. They had one for the road, but not before they were each dragged up to dance two of drunken hen party. The younger cops in the pub thought this was hilarious. Mobile phones were out, no doubt episode of dancing with the stars would be on Facebook within the hour.

Dave managed to escape with a peck on the cheek, Conor however was almost eaten alive by the other drunken woman, who was probably making up for being housebound for the last 6 months.

As he was still trying to get back to his seat Dave got a text, Jackie was outside. He rescued Conor from what seemed like an assault course with him trying to weave in and out of the crowd but was struggling. Dave hadn't noticed until now, just how bad Parkinson's was affecting Conor.

Jackie tried to initiate a conversation with Conor as she drove them home, but he was struggling to stay awake. She remarked to Dave just how tired Conor was.

She later said to Dave that she wasn't surprised at the state of Conor. Although Parkinson's was different for every individual, most sufferers tend to suffer from fatigue, slowness of movement and sufferers can rarely drink alcohol to the extent they used to.

CHAPTER 13

It was six thirty am on Sunday 17th March and Marks was awoken by the phone ringing. It was Dave Black.

'Hello' said Marks sounding like he'd risen from the dead. 'Conor, its Dave. How you doing this morning' said DS Black

'What time is it?'

'Six thirty' DS Black heard Conor sigh and groan as he was obviously attempting to rouse himself from his slumber.

'Conor. It's Dave. Are you alright?'

'Yeah, I'm just knackered'

'How many did we have to drink last night?'

'4 pints'

'4 pints?. Bloody hell. I feel like rank 14.' said Marks

'You seemed to be really struggling last night. Jackie wanted you to stay at ours because she was worried about you. But you were having none of it'

'I'll be fine in 5 minutes'

'Conor, have you thought about doing reduced hours at work?'

'C'mon Dave. So I can't handle the drink like I used to. I'll just stop drinking. It's not as if I drink much or often anyway is it?'

'No you're right. But I think you should seriously consider reduced hours, or even see about getting pensioned off, after all you've got 25 years in. With the extra years they put on your pension you'd get the full whack.'

'Me, retire. Are you serious. What would I do? Play golf? Go and watch United? No thanks'

'Well ok. But if you want to talk about it, anytime. My door's always open.'

'Thanks Dave. See you soon' and Marks put down the phone.

Marks had to summon up all his energy just to make it to the bathroom and back. He felt tense all over. His legs ached. His arms felt heavy and his shoulders felt as if he was literally carrying the world on them. I'll be alright he thought.

When he went to check the timer on the heating, he'd inadvertently switched it off. No wonder he was cold. He thought there wasn't much point in switching it on now, as he was going to make himself a coffee and go to work. He sat at the dining room table in silence watching the steam rise from his coffee while he contemplated life. The coffee tasted great.

He started up the car and drove off to work. He'd only been driving a few minutes when a cat appeared from nowhere, it ran in front of the car, he slammed the brakes on as quick as he could but a hit it. Somehow it ran off. Must've just missed he thought. The female driver behind him had stopped and had approached his car 'Are you alright?' she said.

'Yeah. Yeah I'm fine thanks, I think I stopped in time' said Marks 'It ran off, but I think one of its legs was hanging a funny way.

'Are you sure you're ok, you look a little white' she replied.
'Yeah, really I'm fine thanks for asking' he said.

She politely smiled and returned to her car.

Marks thought he braked in plenty of time. He must have he'd seen the cat from a fair distance. He got back in his car and drove to work. Having thought about it all the way to work, he wondered if he would have to consider not driving.

But that thought quickly went out his head. How would he get to work, get shopping, go anywhere at work or even get to the football.

He went to Dave's office, but he wasn't there. He found him in the incident room.

'Morning sir' although they were good friends, he always called Dave sir in front of his colleagues, such was his respect for him.

'Morning Conor. I'll brief you in my office' said DS Black.
Marks nodded.

Dave wanted to catch up with him and give him the heads up regarding the Chief Constables conversation with him.

Conor thanked him for his support and assured him the last thing he wanted to do was to compromise any investigation.

'Good. Well there's been a development. Information has come in from Crime stoppers stating that a Gordon Harvey lied about his whereabouts the weekend Elaine Dawson was killed.

'Gordon Harvey.... refresh my memory' said Marks.

'He was one of the guys who Elaine Dawson met on a dating app. DC Stones took his statement. He said he'd been with a Sarah Robertson, his girlfriend over the weekend' said Black

'Oh yes now I remember. Didn't she agree that he was with her over the weekend?' 'That may or not be true because according to information received by crime stoppers, she's not his girlfriend, she's a high-class prostitute!'

'I thought she was a Primary School Teacher' said Marks

'According to crime stoppers. She is also a high-class prostitute. Apparently, she doesn't advertise it's purely by word of mouth and it's only people who can afford her £200 an hour.'

'£200. Bloody hell. That doesn't mean he wasn't with her over the weekend though' stated Marks.

'No but we'll need to look into his story because if she is charging £200 an hour. How the hell could he afford to be with her all weekend? Then again if they've lied about their relationship who knows what else they've lied about.' stated Black

Marks asked, 'Is this the first time we've received intelligence of that sort about Robertson?'

'I don't know' said Black 'I'll ask the guys at the Force Intelligence Bureau if they're aware of her.

But you'd thought if they were, we would've executed a warrant by now. Then again, we both know how hard it can be to be granted a warrant sometimes'.

Marks went into the incident room. Laws came into the room to ascertain what duties she could assist with. Marks told her she timed it perfectly because he was looking for someone with experience to go around to Gordon Harvey's house and bring him down to Headquarters.

But as there is insufficient evidence to detain it would have to be on a voluntary basis. This would mean he could refuse to go with the police, and even if he did go to HQ he could leave whenever he wanted to.

Marks contacted DC'S Munro and Milne and instructed them to finish off what they were doing and get around to Sarah Robertson's address and tell her that they have received information that she is prostituting herself.

Ensure she knows that it would be to her benefit to tell the truth about her relationship, if there was one, with Gordon Harvey, and if he really was with her over the weekend Elaine Dawson was murdered.

Highlight the options open to her said Marks. Make sure she knows if she lies and we find out she could face a prison sentence after all it is a murder investigation.

Marks knew Munro and Milne were good officers and would do what he suggested anyway but nonetheless he wanted to make sure everyone knew what was required. As his tutor cop said to him on the first day on the job, don't assume, because it can make an Ass out of u and me. Something he always remembered, and a surprising number of colleagues forgot from time to time.

CHAPTER 14

DC's Munro and Milne attended at Sarah Robertson's home address. Neither claimed to know a great deal about property prices but they suspected if Robertson was indeed supplementing her earnings as a primary school by being a lady of the night, then surely, she'd have picked a better street to reside in.

Not that they knew the area particularly well but judging by the state of some of the gardens in the street, and child's bicycles lying around this wasn't one of Dundee's nicer areas.

They entered the close and went up to the top floor. No name plate on the door on the left, Robertson on the door on the right. The close was clean and graffiti free, which was at least something. They rang the doorbell. Robertson answered. She seemed to be very surprised when they told her they were police officers. She welcomed them in to the flat. It was a small flat but was nicely decorated and it was very clean. She showed them to the living room, 3rd room on the left. 'Do either of you want a coffee or tea?' she asked.
'No thanks' said Milne answering for both.
'What can I help you with today?' asked Robertson.

Milne explained why they were there and highlighted the seriousness of the allegation that she was not only prostituting herself but that she had lied to police in relation to a murder enquiry. A lie that if true, could result in her facing prosecution for helping a murderer escape justice.

She appeared to be horrified at the accusation at first. Then as she obviously thought more about the allegation, she became angry and pressed Munro and Milne to reveal the source. As far as she was concerned, she was a primary school teacher, who was highly thought of, respected and liked at her school.

How could police believe information received from an anonymous source and put any faith in it. From Munro and Milne's experience they saw her point. She had no idea who would say such a thing. However, she understood that the police had to make enquiries about this.

Certainly, as far as Munro and Milne were concerned, she gave them no reason to suspect she was lying. Robertson said she and Harvey had been dating for months and that he was often there at the weekend. She said she had known Harvey for years as they were at high school together.

Munro however, pressed her on how long they had been dating because he had been led to believe that it was weeks, according to Harvey.

For the first time, Robertson appear to stumble, and they could see she was trying to regain her composure. When did he come over on Saturday, what did you do on Saturday night, what was he wearing, did you order a takeaway?

They peppered her with questions, some legitimate questions about what they did others thrown in to unsettle her. Milne asked what they ordered from the Chinese takeaway. Not did you order one, but what did each of you order? Unknown to her, Harvey hadn't said anything about ordering food this was merely to make her think he must have said they ordered Chinese .... what did he tell them?

Munro gave her a few seconds to think of her answer before she said she was going to detain her and question her at Police Headquarters, and that once they found out the truth they would potentially charge her with wasting police time and keep her for court on Monday.

This was the clincher.

She admitted that Harvey was apparently a good friend and that she lied to police to help him. He told her that if police found out that he had pestered Elaine Dawson to be more than friends he would be their main suspect for her murder.

Munro and Milne knew nothing about anyone pestering Elaine Dawson but kept quiet, going along with Robertson by nodding in the right places and pretending to be sympathetic. The reality was they had no sympathy for someone who was trying to protect a possible murderer.

So where had Harvey been over the weekend if he wasn't here thought Munro and Milne. They asked Robertson but she appeared not to know. She'd given him an alibi because she had feelings for him and deep down, she knew he couldn't have murdered anyone.

Munro phoned Marks with an update of what they had found out. He instructed them to leave Robertson where she was for now. If they arrest her for Attempting to Pervert the Course of Justice, she'll get a lawyer at Headquarters, who will tell her to say no comment. At least if she stays where she is, they could potentially use her again, dependent upon what Harvey says.

CHAPTER 15

DS Gold and DC Crighton were tasked with tracing and detaining Gordon Harvey on account of the information they received from Sarah Robertson. They attended at his home address but there was no reply. The house was in darkness and it certainly appeared as if no one was in. It was a Saturday night after all. They asked the control room to say over the radio that CID should be notified if anyone sees him in the town.

They would then decide whether to detain him for Attempting to Pervert the Course of Justice in relation to the false statement he provided to police. If he was extremely drunk then there would be no point in detaining him as they couldn't interview him under these circumstances, and they would waste their detention.

Gold knew that he could only detain a person once for a crime and that period is up to 12 hours only. After this the person must be arrested – if there is further information comes to light that they have committed the crime. However it may be that they will be released pending further enquiries – this is where you have neither gained more evidence that they have committed the crime or gained evidence that proves the didn't commit the crim. In this case you would release the person grounds no longer exist for them to be detained.

Whilst Gold and Crighton were trying to locate Gordon Harvey, DC Campbell was tasked with finding out what information deceased Elaine Dawson's mobile phone had on it. They were hoping there would be evidence of Gordon Harvey's alleged pestering of her for further dates, because depending on the nature of these texts, if they exist, this may prove to be his motive for killing Elaine Dawson, if he did.

Gordon Harvey was traced at home on Sunday 16th March. He said he'd been out with a few mates yesterday but couldn't remember much as he was drunk.

He was detained by Gold and Crighton. When informed he was to be detained, he was pretty cocky, obviously completely unaware of what Sarah had stated to police earlier that day.

He was taken to Headquarters. Marks decided that as they had built up a rapport with Harvey that they should interview him.

Harvey was acting very confident and even refused the services of a solicitor. He was sticking to his story. Gold and Crighton played along, even going through the yes/no spiral of question at the end of an interview. This is where the police confirm details regarding the incident and what the suspects responses were, only to then hit them with details of the crime contradict what the suspect has been saying. Every police officer loved this part of the enquiry. Where you essentially get one over on the bad guy.

Gold and Crighton had finished the yes/no spiral. They looked at each other, then Gold showed her hand. Harvey's demeanour changed instantly. Cockiness – gone, smile – gone, upright posture including the partly looking down his nose at them, thinking I'm getting away with this – gone.

Replaced by a fearful looking, hunched over, timid man, sitting there like a child scolded by his mother for misbehaving.

He admitted asking Sarah Robertson for a massive favour, knowing full well that the poor girl was in love with him, with no care in the world for the predicament he had put her in.

He said he had feared he was going to be the main suspect for the murder due to him previously going on a date with Elaine Dawson and subsequently sending her numerous text messages asking for further dates.

This however, only explained why he asked Sarah to lie on his behalf, it did not tell the anyone where he was or what he did that weekend.

Harvey knew the game was up. He had to tell them the truth, they were going to find out anyway.

CHAPTER 16

Marks updated Black about the development regarding Gordon Harvey. Marks had thought he'd heard it all in his 25 years' experience, but this was a new one on him. Of course, this was assuming Harvey was telling the truth.

The first thing Marks learnt in the job was that women lie better and more easily than men. He recalled one of the first times he and some colleagues went to try and arrest a male wanted on warrant. As they entered the common close of the flat the male was supposed to be in, they encountered 2 women exiting the close. 'Okay Jean see ye later' said the out of breath morbidly obese female to the other female. Quite clearly walking down three flights was taking their toll on the woman.

One of his colleagues had a brief conversation with the slimmer of the female's he had asked which flat they'd come from and she said flat F, the one the male was supposed to reside in. He then asked if they knew the male who resided there. She said she'd never heard of him; he must be the previous tenant because their niece had recently moved in. She never blinked, skipped a heartbeat, stuttered or even broke stride, casually walking outside.

When we knocked on the door, the very guy we were looking for shouted 'come in auntie Jean'. On hearing the door open he said 'did you forget something' he obviously thought his aunt (the slimmer of the women that we passed in the close) had returned.

Black spoke to a colleague from the Force Intelligence Bureau about Sarah Robertson.

They had received a few pieces of intelligence throughout the last year, but it was too infrequent for police to try and obtain a search warrant. If what Harvey was saying was true, and judging by the predicament he was in, he thought it probably was true. Then they had to somehow get into her other flat, by getting her permission to enter.

Marks informed Black. He too had never heard of this. A Primary school Teacher with a double life.

By day wholesome primary school Teacher, tying kids laces, helping them paint, reading to them, teaching them the alphabet and how to count, teaching them the building blocks of life. By night a sultry siren satisfying lonely rich men. No wonder Munro and Milne never found anything, not that they'd looked, and took her word as the truth, they were in the wrong flat. How were they to know she owned the flat across from the one police had traced her in.

According to Harvey. He had been with Robertson the whole weekend covering when Dawson was murdered. But not as her boyfriend, as her pimp. He was apparently her security.

No wonder she lied. Her teaching career would be ruined if people knew this.

Marks though thought there is no great hurry to deal with this aspect of the enquiry because at the end of the day they are dealing with a murder enquiry. This was basically a prostitution offence, although it was Harvey was saying was true then the police could look at seizing Robertson's assets under the Proceeds of Crime Act 2002.

This Act allows police to seize a person's assets when they believe that person has acquired those
assets through illegal activities. This legislation was primarily set up to deprive drug dealers of their assets, however, can also be used for persons believed to be involved in prostitution.

Any monies recovered in must exceed £1000 before it can be seized. This though doesn't have to be in cash. Some of it can be in cash and some in travellers' cheques. If the combined total is more than £1000, police can seize it.

Marks thought this would be relevant in relation to Sarah Robertson, putting to one side the fact that she has lied to police twice during a murder investigation. Unless of course Harvey became their main suspect and from what Marks knew of his involvement he wasn't the person they were looking for. He couldn't explain it, but he knew Harvey wasn't their man.

The days seemed to be going by so fast and yet despite everyone's best efforts they appeared to be struggling to make inroads into the murders.

Whilst conducting enquiries they managed to establish that Elaine Dawson and Alison Trent didn't appear to know one another. This told them that the link between them both was the killer. They also found out that a primary school teacher had a secret life as a high-class prostitute.

Unfortunately they discovered one of their own, PC Scott Young, was having an affair with the first victim, Elaine Dawson, although they did not think he murdered her.

Marks ascertained that he would have to acquire the services of a solicitor in order to handle the Power of Attorney issue surrounding his mother to stop his brother potentially taking advantage of her. Marks was feeling more lethargic by the day.

CHAPTER 17

Jill Williams was a young Belfast girl who chose to study in Dundee due to its good universities and because she got a good vibe from it when she came over for a weekend to check out what was in the city. Despite both her and Fiona coming from Belfast they met for the first time at Dundee University student's union at a Freshers week party. They were best friends as well as partners.

Jill was the quiet one of the two. She had wanted to become a primary teacher since she was a child. She thought that this was where you can make the most impact on a child.

She was thrilled when she passed her teaching course and was ecstatic when she was posted to Linlathen Primary School. She'd spent some time at the school on a secondment for three months and got on well with the children and with the staff. This was her first choice of school when she had graduated.

She would phone home two or three times a week to speak to her mother who she was incredibly close to. It wasn't that she wasn't close with her dad, but it was her mother who had always taken her to Sunday school, girl guides, piano practice and badminton. Her dad took her occasionally but often he was either working or taking her younger brother to his karate.

She doted on David, her younger brother. It was Jill that taught him how to read. But David had recently passed his driving test, which meant he was hardly ever in when she phoned. But he texts her daily.

Although she loved teaching, she was looking forward to going home to see her family at Easter.

About 1430hrs Friday 22nd March. The control room received a phone call from a hysterical woman on the other end of the phone. It took all of Sergeant Martin's experience to obtain the smallest piece of information from her.

There had been another Murder.

She had come home from seeing her parents in Belfast and had found her flatmate dead in her room. Blood everywhere.

Although uniform officers were asked to attend, CID were also notified. CID officers were the first on the scene, largely due to being on enquiries nearby.

When DC's Munro and Milne arrived at locus they were met by several people outside the locus.

Some of the people were attempting to calm the distraught woman, whilst others looked on helplessly.

Uniformed officers arrived soon after CID and whilst one officer tried to calm the distraught female down, the other stood guard at the flat using his notebook as a makeshift Crime Scene Log.

The two detectives entered the locus. There was blood on the first few feet of the walls of the hall, not much but some.

To them it looked like someone had been hit as the droplets of blood seemed to be in a spattered and not in a pool. They walked down the hall and noticed there appeared to be a faint bloodied footprint at the far end of the hall, just before they reached the living room. They stepped over the footprint and entered the living room. Through the living room which led onto another smaller hall. They could see there was the odd drip of blood leading from this hall into the first room on the right.

There were another 2 doors in this hall They put gloves on, so that they wouldn't leave their fingerprints on anything. They entered the first room on the right.

There was a naked female lying on her right side. There was a lot of blood all over the bed. They couldn't see her face. They saw her wrists had been tied together with cord, but her ankles had no marks on them. The fingers on both hands were missing. Munro checked for a pulse trying her best not to stand in the blood around the bed. But she couldn't find one. They noted that it looked like she'd been strangled. They retreated to the front door, treading carefully, trying not to disturb anything, including deceased's clothing which was strewn across the room.

Once they had established the victim was dead, there was no need to go any further into the flat. Secure the locus and let the Scenes of Crime Officers do their stuff, they'd been taught.

Cumming updated the control room whilst Milne updated Marks. Marks had to notify the Detective Superintendent of this latest development.

DS Laws was appointed CSM for this murder.

Laws and DC Martin attended at locus. They put Forensic suits on and entered the flat. Martin began filming as Laws narrated. They entered the hallway, filming the blood spattered on the wall.

Laws thought it looked like, someone, most probably deceased, had been punched and that this created the blood spatters on the wall. She also noticed droplets of blood from the hall went beyond the door.

They also noticed there was a faint partial footprint of blood on the hall, before they reached the door. The droplets of blood led them from the hall, through the living room and into deceased's bedroom.

They opened the door and saw deceased lying naked on her right side. They couldn't see her face. Her wrists tied together with cord. Her ankles, however, hadn't been tied together. Why didn't she have her ankles tied? Maybe he was able to control her more easily and didn't need to do that, thought Laws. Her fingers on both hands had been cut off.

There was a lot of blood on the bed. Laws thought there was no way the killer has not left a fingerprint or DNA somewhere in here, there's too much blood for him not to have meet it.

They filmed deceased's badly bruised neck, it looked like she'd been strangled thought Laws. It also looked like she had a broken nose. This would explain the blood on the hallway walls. She was probably punched by the killer as she opened the door.

She also noted that deceased had sustained a burn mark at the front right side of her shoulder. The burn looked like two small dots.

Laws had previously spoke to Budd in the office about the murders of Elaine Dawson and Alison Trent in which he mentioned both had a burn mark on their shoulder and neck respectively. This sealed it for Laws, this was the same killer.

She saw a bloody footprint, a partial one, but even still, that was potentially a good piece of evidence. She showed Martin the partial print and told him to make sure he got that on film. She would take the partial print. They had plenty of swabs of blood. They had lots of tape taken from deceased's face and neck, taking for DNA purposes. They finished off filming.

Laws then contacted Marks and updated him.
Marks ordered her to lockdown the scene. He was in a meeting with DS Black and the Chief
Constable Pamela Harkins. But he stated that as soon as they were finished, he and DS Black would attend the scene. He also stated that he would contact the force doctor and have her attend.
Marks hadn't had many conversations with Harkins but had found her to amiable and respectful of her senior officers' opinions.

She was recently divorced from her husband who was also a high-ranking police officer. That's probably why she came to Tayside, he thought, to get some space from him.

It wasn't always the way when Tayside Police had promoted an officer from outwith the area to Chief Constable that their opinions were taken on board. So many of the officers appointed Chief Constable have come to Tayside to use the post as a stepping stone to other bigger forces. Although Tayside Police were small compared to other divisions around Britain, it was an area with its fair share of problems, and one that would be relatively easy to increase the detection rates and make someone look good.

Everyone knew that if you throw enough resources at a problem it will inevitably decrease, detection rates will go up, and the person whose brainchild it was will be a shining light.

There was a time when Marks would say what he thought about anything, but he kept these thoughts to himself now. He's no longer the naive Detective Constable that would often speak his mind, being oblivious to the fact the on occasions he was criticising the very people whose ideas were being implemented in their effort to show they should get promoted.

Harkins was concerned, she wanted fully briefed on where they were in all investigations, albeit she was aware the latest one was ongoing. She had been briefed on the murder of Elaine Dawson and was about to be briefed on the murder of Alison Trent when they were informed about the discovery of victim number three. Three murders. She'd only been appointed Chief Constable a few months ago.

Still, she thought, this will look good for me, if we catch this guy quickly.

Marks and Black attended at locus.

They decided they would get kitted out in the Forensic suits straight away and get in there, rather than wait on Dr Dempster, after all they didn't know how long she was going to be. This would also give DS Black the chance to update the Chief Constable as soon as.

They met DS Laws and DC Martin outside deceased's home. Once they were suited up, they walked through the flat guided by Laws who was telling them where they had taken samples of blood, saliva, footprints and fingerprints from. They could see the dust where they had taken fingerprints from, shoe prints and footprints from.

They noted deceased was a small girl, about 5ft 2, slight build, long black hair. She looked very similar to the first victim Elaine Dawson, he thought. She had bruising all around her wrists where she'd been bound. Marks was surprised at the amount of blood in the bedroom, because there didn't appear to be that much in the previous two crime scenes. Deceased's clothing was scattered around the room. They left it where it was. The CSM would take these for forensic evidence when he was ready.

The killer would have blood on their clothing he thought. There's simply too much blood for him not to have gotten some of it on himself.

Also, why had the killer cut off all her fingers when he had only cut off the fingers of one hand from the first two victims.

Dr Dempster had arrived. She knocked on the bedroom door at the same time DS Black and DCI Marks were about to leave. Marks and Black stayed whilst the doctor briefly examined deceased. As before she thought strangulation was the cause of death but stated that deceased would have died relatively quickly in any case due to the amount of blood loss from her fingers being cut off.

She noticed that she had a broken nose also. But that she may have managed to punch the killer before he subdued her judging by her bruised knuckles. She suspected as both Marks and Black had, that she had been raped after death also.

The timescale in which the killer was striking was worrying Marks. Three murders in 3 weeks.
DC Milne had taken a statement from Fiona O'Neill, the girl who had found her girlfriend and flat mate Jill Williams dead.

She spoke to deceased late on the Thursday night, around 11pm, when she phoned her to tell her she was getting in between 2 and 3 pm tomorrow. She said Jill mentioned that Police were at the door and that she had to go.

Milne excused himself and contacted Marks. They may have a specific time in which the killer may be caught on camera, not only that, Williams said police were at her door. If the killer is posing as a police officer, then that's going to cause them major issues. There were a lot of cameras near to the locus due to it being near the city centre.

Once more Marks checked the police computer system for calls to the locus or flats surrounding it. But it was to no avail. He was deeply concerned by this. He wanted his officers to concentrate on cctv and house to house in their efforts to unmask this monster. Marks wondered if the killer was becoming more confident in his ability to kill his victims and evade police.

He was thinking this because he had taken precautions in limiting his first two victims' chances of screaming by stuffing an object into their mouth. However on the slim chance they did scream, it would be difficult to locate where the person was screaming was, due to the number of flats in the area and there being very few people walking about. Whereas on this occasion, the flat was so central, and in amongst a host of student flats, that surely somebody would have heard something and raised the alarm.

Price also found out that deceased was gay and that her girlfriend was the hysterical female she had encountered on his attendance at the scene.

She was only 24 and worked at Linlathen Primary School, where she had worked for the past two years. Deceased originated from Belfast too.

Officers from the Police Service of Northern Ireland would have to be notified in order to pass the death message to her parents. They would also have to provide their equivalent of a Family Liaison Officer.

All detective officers and an army of uniform officers were now assembled in a packed canteen.

There was far too many to brief in an incident room. The canteen had been closed to anyone for the time being not involved in enquiries related to the murder.

The briefing was short. The priority was house to house enquiries for any flats in the same street as deceased's, any flats overlooking deceased's (There were quite a lot of these) and cctv reviews of any cameras near to Williams' flat for anyone wearing a hat, even one that looked like a policeman's hat.

Also, there was a good chance the person would have blood on their clothing or maybe nursing a bloody face and/or carrying a bag. The thinking behind this was, as Dr Dempster stated the killer may have been punched by Williams, so he may have sustained a bloody face. Whilst it wasn't a great deal to go on, because they felt they had the time the murderer arrived at locus, it would make their task a lot easier.

All cctv reviews were to be carried out by detective officers instructed Marks. The reason behind this was that they wanted it kept secret that the killer may be a police officer or may be impersonating a police officer and it was easier to do this if fewer people knew.

Once again Dr Dempster was conducting the post-mortem and once again Tommy was filming it.

The time is 1pm Sunday 24th March. Deceased is Jill Williams, born 14/12/94.

Present are DS Black, DCI Marks, DS Laws, DC Martin, myself – Dr Dempster and my assistant Tommy Turner.

As was the case with the previous murders, cause of death was established as manual strangulation.

Deceased had all her fingers cut off and would have died within minutes due to severe blood loss had she not been strangled.

However, the angle of the cuts indicates they've been cut by a person using his left hand which differs from the other murders where the killer is right-handed.

'So, we could have two killers loose in the city?' said Marks. 'Possibly but not necessarily' said Dempster.

Like Elaine Dawson and Alison Trent she also had an item stuffed into her throat prior to her death, which the killer had removed. Also, she has a burn mark consisting of two small holes roughly an inch in length apart on her right shoulder.

There are marks on deceased's left knuckles indicating that she punched something or someone a short time prior to her death.

The post-mortem also revealed that like the previous victims, deceased had been raped prior to and after death.

The whiteboard now had three victims' names on it,

1st. Elaine Dawson, b. 14/02/77, single, lawyer – 64 Kings Ave, Dundee, 5ft 8, slim, short black hair,

2nd. Alison Trent, b. 04/04/93, single, personal trainer – 41 Barnes Rd, Dundee, 5ft 5, slim, long blonde hair

3rd. Jill Williams, b. 14/12/94, single, teacher – 11 Prospect Place, Dundee, 5ft, 2, slim, long dark hair

All three strangled and raped.
DNA found on first two victims. Awaiting results of 3rd PM

No suspects. No link found suggesting all three knew each other.

CHAPTER 18

Detective Superintendent Black was handling this press release. Not that anyone thought Marks had done something wrong, but simply it would look like police were putting more resources into the murders and had instructed one of its top cops to oversee the investigation. Marks was too long in the tooth to worry about it. He knew fine well why Black was doing the press release. He was however, determined to catch this killer before he struck again.

Black held the press conference and Marks had to admit he was brilliant at it. Looked very assured in what he was saying, never panicked, was always in control and he answered the questions asked of him without giving anything away. He could be a politician thought Marks. He had the art of saying nothing whilst giving the impression he was saying everything.

Like before the journalists were determined to obtain every ounce of information they could about the investigations. As before, however, they would go away knowing a little more than before they came in but that's it.

Marks and Thompson were sitting in his office having a general chat during a brief break in the tidal wave of questions they were being asked in the incident room. Thompson was eager to put his stamp on these murder enquiries and get himself noticed. Marks liked his ambition and the way he was going about it, but he was also thinking it could help him get one last promotion before he retires and the promotion from Chief Inspector to Superintendent was where the biggest jump in the pension was. Not that Marks bothered about money. He'd always worked that many hours that he hardly had time to spend his cash. Besides he never had kids or even a wife to spend money on.

There had been women in his life, but they were a distant second to his work.

Again his thoughts turned to the idea of finding a woman and building a relationship with a woman and see what develops from there he thought. After all he only had 5 years left to work in the police and the thought of being stuck in the house on his own day after day didn't appeal to him.

CHAPTER 19

DC Price was carrying out enquiries with deceased Alison Trent's friends when she traced Karen Bell. She hadn't seen Alison for a few weeks but did state that she dated Kevin Ferguson for 6 months, prior to Alison dating him. This initially caused a bit of tension between the two, but they soon made up. She stated that she warned Alison about Kevin. This took Price by surprise because she was led to believe, having spoken to Paula Crighton, that Kevin was a friendly, likeable man, not to mention hunky.

She was intrigued. 'What do you mean you warned her about Kevin?' she asked.

'Everybody thinks Kevin is the perfect man because he's very attractive, got a great body, and has money, but he likes to control everything you do. We were dating for 6 months and by the end of the six months he was checking my text messages every night I said I was working late. He even downloaded an app on my phone to track where I was' said Karen.

'Once, when I was waiting to meet him, he turned up as I was speaking to an old school friend. He went ballistic, why was I speaking to him, is he an old boyfriend, are you sleeping with him. I thought 'Fuck off' who do you think you are?' I told him to stop the car.'

He wouldn't stop the car, shouting nobody leaves me, look at me I can get any girl I want; you should be grateful getting a guy like me. I asked him to stop but he said no we need to talk. I got out when we were stuck in traffic at traffic lights in the town. He tried to come over to my house later that night, but my brother was in, so he didn't hang about.

'Why?' asked Price.

'Because he knows my brother would leather him. My brother Paul teaches Krav Maga and he knows this, and he knows my brother is very protective.

He was fine the first 4 months we went out until he starting using steroids. That's when he became possessive and controlling. I stayed with him for two months after that, then when we had that argument about me talking to an old schoolfriend that was it. I've never even spoke to him since.

'Was he ever violent to you?' asked Price. 'No. Like I said he knows my brother would leather him if he was' she said.

Price thanked Karen for her time and returned to Headquarters.

Amy Hart phoned Marks. She had the results from the Jill Willliams crime scene. They had recovered a specimen of blood from the hall where the killer appears to have been hit by her as he entered the property.

She also had a partial footprint obtained from the bedroom which indicated the person was a size 10 in a shoe/boot.

She further stated that she had ran the blood sample through the database but there was no match to anyone in the database. There was a fingerprint recovered from the hall, near to where the blood was found but that too hasn't come back to anyone in the database. But at least they have them to compare against someone's when they have a suspect.

CHAPTER 20

Marks, Black, and Thompson met Chief Constable Harkins to discuss all three murders and what suspects if any were in the frame for each one. Who had a motive to kill all three? Who would be capable of doing this and who had the opportunity?

'Let's start with the evidence we've got. What do we have?' asked Harkins.

'Well. We got DNA from Elaine Dawson's body. 2 different people, one of whom is Scott Young.

He's the cop that was having an affair with Dawson. But when we spoke to him, he did say he had gone up there for sex. He left having been up there for about 40 minutes. The other came back is not known to anyone in the National Database.

'So, he was the last one to see her alive?' asked Harkins looking for clarification.
'Yes' replied Marks.
'So he's the last one to see her alive, his DNA is on or in the victim rather. Does he have an alibi for the other two murders?' said Harkins.

'We haven't spoken to him yet about the other two.' said Marks.

Both Harkins and Black looked astonished. Not that police officers didn't have affairs, because if they were all being honest, they would say it was very common amongst police officers. But that he
didn't come forward with that information, as soon as the murder was discovered. Unless of course he had something to hide.

Marks stated 'Apparently now, he's residing with his mother because his wives kicked him out.

This is also his reason for him not having an alibi for the rest of the time covering the period Elaine Dawson may have been killed'.

Nobody has spoken to him regarding the Trent or Williams murders because we haven't been able to establish yet if he knows them'.

'Well that's a priority' said Harkins. 'Because if it turns out he's responsible, and I'm not saying he is, but on the slim chance that he is responsible we need to find this out because the press will have a field day and our careers will be down the toilet'.

Marks continued. There's Gordon Harvey. He's the guy that lied to us about his whereabouts over the weekend Elaine Dawson was killed. He claimed to have been with his girlfriend Sarah Robertson, who later admitted he made this up so that we wouldn't think he was a suspect. He thought he would be our main suspect because he pestered Elaine Dawson for another date after she spurned him after their initial date' stated Marks.

'It now transpires that he made it up to protect Robertson, as well as himself of course, because he is apparently her pimp' said Marks in a surprised tone of voice.

Although he sounded surprised it was nothing compared to the reaction given by Harkins, who by now was sitting back in her chair cross legged with her arms folded. Her eyes widened, she inhaled through the nose and then let out an enormous sigh.

Marks thought, she's thinking what the hell, is this considered normal behaviour in Dundee. We are still awaiting the results of Elaine Dawson's laptop being examined. Her phone has been examined but there isn't anything incriminating on it. There are texts from him but it's nothing of any real concern.

Harkins replied, 'So we have two possible for the Dawson murder, anymore?' Marks answered, there's only one more now.

Kevin Ferguson. He had recently started having a relationship with Alison Trent. Paula Crighton spoke to him and she thought he was genuine. I think Paula is a good judge of character but according to Karen Bell, who was one of Trent's good friends, she split up with Ferguson because of his possessive and controlling behaviour. Although she did say he never hit her, she did say that could've been because he knows her brother Paul teaches Krav Maga and that he is very protective of her.

We haven't spoken to him about any of the murders, although when Paula Crighton spoke to him, he said he was home alone over the time period Alison Trent was murdered.

Are any of these three physically capable of committing these murders, bearing in mind the skills they'd have needed in order to subdue a fit, young female who was proficient in Krav Maga?' asked Harkins.

'Well Gordon Harvey doesn't look particularly big or fit, but if he used a stun gun or taser, like we suspect the killer did then possibly. Also, when we were carrying out enquiries into the murder of Alison Trent, we learned that he sold her the flat she was living in. So, he knew her. Although at this moment in time we don't have a motive. We don't know if he knew Jill Williams' said Marks 'We definitely need to speak to him to find out where he was covering the periods where Trent and Williams were murdered' stated Harkins.

He didn't have an alibi for the period when Dawson was killed. Claims to have been out with friends the night Trent was murdered and was in custody for some of the time period when Williams was killed, albeit he still could've killed her before traced by police. 'Anyone else in the frame for the murders?' said Harkins

There's Kevin Ferguson. He's a Bank Manager. He recently started having a relationship with Alison Trent. He also arranged the mortgage for Dawson to buy her flat, so he knew her. We haven't spoken to him regarding Williams. He is, according to an ex-girlfriend Karen Bell said to be possessive, controlling and has a temper. He is very muscular and would have no problem handling all three deceased.

'We don't know if he has a motive though?' said Harkins.

Scott Young, PC, was having an affair with Dawson. He knew Alison Trent from the gym she worked at because he is a member there and takes some of her classes. He also knew Jill Williams, as she is one of his daughter's schoolteacher. He was working for some of the time when Dawson was murdered and hid the fact, he had sex with her over the weekend she was murdered. Was apparently staying at his mother's address alone, whilst she was on holiday. As a result of the affair. He was also on his own the night Trent was killed at his mother's address where they detained him for the murder of Elaine Dawson.

He was working the night Williams was killed. Although he was apparently sent home from work because he was sick.

There's nobody else in the frame now.

Black had been sitting taking everything in, no notes needed. He had a memory like a computer he remembered names, dates, events like he was reading them.

'What about this guy Paul Bell, that Karen, the ex of Kevin Ferguson mentioned. She said he was her brother and that he taught Krav Maga. If he taught Krav Maga he would have known Alison Trent. It would be worth speaking to him to find out if Alison talked about problems with ex boyfriends, or Kevin Ferguson, her latest boyfriend. She may have turned up every week with someone else. He would have the skills to subdue Trent, Dawson and Williams'.

'Wait a minute, Paul Bell, Paul Bell, Paul Bell, where do I know that name from?' said a puzzled Marks, who was now pacing the room with his right hand up to his chin, only taking his fingers off momentarily to raise them up to his head to scratch it. Searching the depths of his brain for the information he knew was in there but was struggling to recall. I know. As he said this he pointed to Black.

He was one of the two people who met Elaine Dawson after arranging a date through a dating app.

That's it. They only went out once and she didn't want to go on another date because there was something about him that made her feel uneasy. As far as I know he didn't bother her after that. I'll need to find out who spoke to him and get someone to contact him and arrange a meet' said a triumphant Marks. Pleased with himself that he managed to recall a vital piece of information.

These days remembering anything beyond what happened after breakfast was an achievement.

Harkins spoke 'right we need to speak to him, also as a matter of urgency. We also need to establish firstly if it was indeed him and not another Paul Bell. If he has a motive and where he was over the three periods each of the women was killed.

Marks also stated that he would like to ascertain the movements of the concierge who was seen on camera walking about the building Elaine Dawson resided in after midnight.

Although he'd been informed by Mason that according to the supervisor this is not uncommon.

Apparently if the security team are busy then the concierge within the office can and does on occasions check the buildings for security reasons.

'So' Harkins had the floor. 'We really need to get Paul Bell in here and the concierge Purvis spoken to and begin eliminating them from the enquiries. From what you've told me Conor we have at least 1 strong subject that we can consider a suspect in Bell. Tracing him is the priority.

At that the Chief Constable ended their meeting.

CHAPTER 21

Marks returned to the incident room and briefed his team of detectives.

DC's Crighton and Price were tasked with tracing Scott Young and detaining him for the murder of Elaine Dawson due to the fact he openly stated he was with her the night it's believed she was murdered.

DC's Munro and Milne were tasked with tracing Kevin Ferguson and persuading him to attend HQ to be questioned. They did not have enough evidence currently to detain him. The only problem with this is that even if he comes to HQ on a voluntary basis he can leave whenever he likes. Unless he says something that incriminates himself, they would need to let him go.

DC's Mason and Kelly had been tasked to trace Bell. However, as was the case with Ferguson they would need to persuade him to accompany them to HQ.

Immediately, Mason and Kelly set to work researching all police systems in order to establish addresses he could be at, family, friends he could be with, phone numbers he had, vehicles he was driving and places he frequented.

Marks knew Gordon Harvey and Neil Purvis would have to spoke to again, but he thought what happens if they trace everyone they're needing to speak to at once. That would leave them trying to juggle speaking to 5 suspects whilst they would probably be learning new information all the time throughout the interviews.

He knew what the priorities were, after all, he'd had his orders from the Chief Constable herself. Besides, as desperate as they were to catch the killer this was something they couldn't rush, or it could lead to mistakes happening.

CHAPTER 22

YOUNG

Crighton and Price traced Scott Young at his mother's address where they detained him for the murder of Elaine Dawson. His mother was in disbelief "he's one of you for Christ's sake. How could you think he would murder anyone?' To be fair to Scott he told her they were just doing their job. Although he too was surprised at being detained, he knew he had nothing to worry about.

He was placed in the back of the unmarked car but wasn't handcuffed. They knew he posed no threat to them, so they chose not to handcuff him. They took him to HQ.

The custody suite was on lockdown from the moment they arrived. They were aware that people gossip especially in the police and they didn't want anyone outside of the people who were at Marks' briefing knowing what was happening.

They kept Young in the car until the custody suite was clear of any other prisoners, uniform staff and police personal that weren't necessary to book Young in.

When they booked him through custody, they immediately took him upstairs and into an interview room where DC Price remained with him. Although Young knew his rights due to the seriousness of the allegation, he wanted a solicitor present. His solicitor attended within the hour, which was quick.

DS Gold and DI Thompson were conducting the interview.

Throughout the whole process Young was quiet and at times appeared miles away. Then again, as he told Crighton and Price on the way to Headquarters, he had lost everything. His wife had kicked him out and was unwilling to let him see his daughter whom he doted on. He was living with his mother, who made it abundantly clear she thought he was an idiot for what he'd done. Although he was her son and she would always be there for him he made a big mistake. He ruined the best things in his life and his mother wasn't going to let him forget it. She was also suffering because she was no longer getting to see her granddaughter, at least for the time being.

Young's solicitor quite often told him to say no comment, however Young, answered the questions openly and confidently, much to his solicitor's annoyance. He appeared to have no worries with the fact he was the last one to see Elaine Dawson alive. believed him when he said he knew nothing about the killing because he seemed to be carefree.

They then asked him about the murders of Alison Trent and Jill Williams. He had no alibi for the murder of Trent. As he had stated previously, he'd been home alone, at his mother's address whilst she was on holiday. However, on the date Williams was murdered he was at his mother's home address with his mother who returned from holiday by this time. This would be easy to check out.

They broke off the interview and informed Marks.

Marks fully trusted Thompson and Gold's judgement. Nonetheless, as expected, he asked Gold to confirm with Young's mother if he had in fact been with her on the night of the 22nd March. She confirmed this. She remembers specifically because she had been to the funeral of an ex colleague.

Once Marks received confirmation that Young indeed had an alibi, he eliminated him as a suspect and released him from his detention.

Before he left, they informed him that with regards to him having sex whilst on duty, this would be discussed by the Chief Superintendent for Dundee and the professional standards Chief Inspector later.

They never said to him, although they think he knew, his days were numbered in the police force.

Marks popped in to see DC's Mason and Kelly to see how the cctv reviews were progressing in relation to the Williams murder. Kelly had managed to obtain a good image on a neighbours' private cctv of a male, wearing a hat, carrying a bag walking away from the vicinity of Williams' flat.

Neither Mason nor Kelly knew this man. Mason did think however, he was the same height and build of the unidentified male from the cctv footage they had obtained from Elaine Dawsons building.

The time of this image was just after midnight on the 22nd March.

This would tie in with the time that her girlfriend last spoke to her.

'Get that image on Can U Id as soon as possible and give me a copy of the photo and I'll speak to Dave Black about getting this out to the press' said Marks.

The image was placed on the web page for a few hours only, before they had a positive reply.
DC Fyffe worked in Aberdeen but had seen the Can u Id images that Mason had placed on the website. He couldn't be one hundred percent sure because when he'd last seen him, he was only 12, which was 12 years ago, but he thought one of the images was that of Mathew Davie. He couldn't recall his date of birth off the top of his head, but he had researched the police systems and discovered it was 2nd March 1995.

He'd had the misfortune of dealing with his father's accident many years ago when he was killed in a road accident. Then again, a month and years later when Mathew went off the rails. He'd butchered his guinea pigs in the back garden. A while after that he'd killed several cats over a weekend stringing them up and disembowelling them. He was lucky not to have been lynched. The locals were baying for his blood and if it wasn't for his uncle Terry smoothing things over then things would've turned nasty for sure. That was until he was found to be responsible for the fire that destroyed a factory in Aberdeen. The factory fire caused the factory to close resulting in over one hundred people losing their jobs.

The other children at school would keep well clear of him. He was always playing on his own because of this. He was never invited to their parties, sleepovers or any social events because the kids were so scared of him. Even his teachers weren't keen to be left alone with him. His strange and uncaring attitude left people with the opinion that he shouldn't be in mainstream schooling.

Eventually even his uncle Terry Bell had enough. The last straw was when he caught him spying on his young daughter playing with her friends, whilst he was masturbating. The girls were all under ten. He put Mathew up for adoption.

Although Terry never made an official complaint to police about the incident Terry himself had told people what happened, and Mathew never denied it. Terry placed him up for adoption.

DC Fyffe didn't know who adopted him, but he knew it was outside Aberdeen, possibly Forfar but he couldn't be sure. He knew Mathew was a ticking time bomb. He wouldn't be surprised if he changed his name thought Fyffe. After all, anyone who knew his history wouldn't associate themselves with him or take a chance in hiring him.

Fyffe put all this information in an email to Mason, which was greatly appreciated by Marks and his team. All they had to do now was trace Mathew Davie or whoever he was now.

CHAPTER 23

After a lot of enquiries had been carried out with numerous foster families, police eventually found the last foster home Mathew Davie had resided at. Despite having fostered over 20 children throughout the years Derek and Donna Higgins could still recall Mathew Davie. He was over 6ft and quite stocky even at 16 and despite only staying with them for a matter of weeks they remembered him due to his violent behaviour. They thought he might be bipolar and wanted him to go for testing to see if this was the case, but he declined and became quite angry at this. When Derek went to have a word with him in his room, he punched Derek, knocking him out and knocking out a couple of his teeth in the process.

They never made an official complaint to police because he left right after this and they never saw him again.

However, Derek saw him working as a doorman about a year later at a pub. He was out with friends and asked him how he was doing. Mathew however, said he must have the wrong person because his name was Paul something.

Derek thought he said Paul Bell, but he could be mistaken.

Mason immediately contacted Marks to inform him of this.

Marks had recalled that DC Price had spoken to Karen Bell and her brother being called Paul. Coincidence. Well a phone call to Karen Bell would clarify matters. But Marks thought it might be better to get Price who she spoke to originally to speak to her as she'd built up a rapport with her already, and this may make her more likely to divulge information about him.

Nonetheless he was going to make enquiries with Deed Poll to ascertain if Paul Bell used to be called Mathew Davie. He could also do a voter roll check to see where he is residing now, however this may return more than one address, after all there's probably more than one Paul Bell in the area, thought Marks.

Meanwhile Munro and Milne traced Neil Purvis at his home address. He was quite happy to speak to police about his movements. He stated that he did enter Elaine Dawson's building in the early hours of Saturday 2nd March because the mobile security team were busy elsewhere and he thought he'd seen someone enter the building who he didn't know.

Munro asked him if he was concerned why didn't he go there with a colleague so that there would be less chance of him getting assaulted if he did trace an unwanted visitor to the flats. Purvis however, revealed that he was a Krav Maga instructor along with 2 other men who ran the Dundee club. 'What are the names of the other two men?' asked Milne.

'Paul Bell and Calum Watson' stated Purvis.

'Did you trace anyone in the building?' asked Munro.

'No' said Purvis

'You must've been pretty sure someone went in if you went from your office to the flats' said Munro. 'I was. I checked the cctv footage when I returned to the office and I saw a male, at least I think it was a man enter about 1'o'clock in the morning. He was carrying a bag. Although the image isn't great of the person, I didn't recognise his height and build as being that of anyone I knew in the building.'

'Could he have got out the building without you seeing?'

'Yeah. He could've got out one of the fire escapes at the back of the building. Or he could have left between the time I left the office and I arrived at the building, but I checked to see if I could see him leaving when I returned to the office but if he left he didn't leave through the front door.'

'Where does the fire escapes lead to?' asked Munro

'The rear of the building which leads to a car park of another block of flats in Woodside Avenue which is the street behind Kings Avenue' replied Purvis

'Do you know if you can walk out of there into the street?'

Purvis nodding his head said 'Yeah, there's a path that leads onto Woodside Avenue'

'Where were you on the night of the 14th March?' asked Munro. "I was at my sister's house. My sister was taking her husband for a meal because it was his birthday, so I watched the boys to let them out.' 'And what time did they return?' 'About 11pm. I left almost as soon as they come in, coz I figured they'd want some time to themselves. I went home watched some tv and went to bed' 'And where were you on the Thursday 22nd March?' 'At work. Well I finished at 1am. I went home and went to bed'

'That's great Mr Purvis thanks for your help. We'll be in touch if we need anything else' said Munro. 'Yeah no problem'

Munro and Milne left. They were both satisfied that Purvis was telling the truth.

They asked him if he was willing to provide a sample of DNA to be compared with DNA they had found at the murders. He agreed. 'No problem' he said.

They returned to HQ and updated Marks. He seemed satisfied that they believed Purvis. Slowly but surely, they were whittling down the suspects. Now they were down to Paul Bell and Kevin Ferguson, although he wasn't sure about Ferguson.

He rated Paula Crighton quite highly when it came to being a good judge of character, so to hear that he was apparently a possessive and controlling person didn't seem quite right to him. Albeit, he was aware everyone can have the wool pulled over the eyes sometimes. It was starting to look like this Paul Bell was the man they were after.

His gut was telling him he was the man they were looking for.

DC's Crighton and Price traced Kevin Ferguson at his home address. He was surprised to see them and even more surprised when they asked him to accompany them to HQ. He agreed to go with them to police headquarters but wasn't too happy about it.

Marks was informed they were end route to HQ with Ferguson.

He contacted Price through his radio asking her to come into his office before he filled out the voluntary attendance forms.

When they arrived Price stated to Crighton that she could fill out the paperwork as she had something she needed to do before they got started.

She went to Marks' office and was told to put Ferguson in interview room 1 where Marks had set up the cctv for him to view what Ferguson was saying in reply to the questions they were asking and to observe his body language.

Price then went to get Crighton and Ferguson and tell them where they were going. She took them to interview room 1 as instructed by DCI Marks.

They cautioned him and reminded him that he could leave at any time, but he was wanting the matter resolved once and for all.

He stated that he was friends with Elaine Dawson and had been for years as both his mum and her mum had been friends for years. He saw her as a good family friend and how her murder had ripped the heart out of her mother and father. He said he too was upset over her death and how he hoped the killer would be brought to justice.

So far, Marks hadn't seen or heard anything that would lead him to the conclusion that Ferguson was lying and was the kind of man Karen Bell stated he was.

The interview continued and as far as Marks was concerned nothing changed for him. He thought Ferguson came across as genuine and although he didn't have an alibi that could be corroborated for any of the murders, his gut was telling him he wasn't the man they were after. The body language of Ferguson was indicating he was telling the truth also. He was confident with his answers, his eyes didn't wander from the eyeline of the interviewers, he never stuttered or stumbled with his words or shifted in his seat. Nothing, from what he was seeing was giving Marks cause for concern.

He knocked on the door of the interview room.

Price came out. 'Ask him if he is willing to provide a sample of DNA to be compared with DNA found at the scene and see what he says' said Marks.

Sure enough, as Marks thought. He had no objection to this in fact he thought it was a good idea because that would clear him from being brought down to headquarters again.

He provided a DNA sample and could leave. Marks was so confident he had nothing to do with the murders he would stake his reputation on it.

They would know the result of the DNA comparison by tomorrow afternoon.

CHAPTER 24

Enquiries were carried out with Deed Poll regarding Paul Bell. Fortunately once the correct paperwork was submitted, they informed the police that there was a Mathew Davie who changed his name to Paul Bell. His date of birth was 2nd March 1995 born in Aberdeen. His last address according to them was given as an address in Aberdeen.

Marks knew this would be an old address and had DC Mason conduct a voter roll check for him in the Tayside area, however, this did not yield any results. He then checked police systems including the system the control room use to try an establish where Paul Bell was. However, if he was in the area, he didn't register himself as a voter, nor had he reported or been reported for any crimes or incidents to the police.

Marks was frustrated. It appeared as if Bell was always one step ahead of them.

Marks thought they can make enquiries with Krav Maga club and see is they know where he is staying but he's probably put a fake address. At the end of the day they can ascertain when the classes are and turn up waiting for him. They would then be able to quickly establish if he is the male they are looking for.

Marks' phone rung. It was Amy Hart from the Forensic labs again. Bad news, the two samples given by Kevin Ferguson and Neil Purvis were not a match to the DNA samples they had already recovered. Marks thanked her for her efforts and thought at least he could rule them out now. He also thought, this is good because they could allocate more resources on tracing Paul Bell.

Price was out and about on enquiry when she saw Karen Bell from a distance. As she got closer to her she recognised the male with her. This was the male that was in the Can U Id photos. She was about to contact the control room to request they get further units to attend in the area when she saw them get into a black Nissan Qashqai. She noted the registration number and requested the control room carry out a registered keeper check on the vehicle.

However this came back as registered to a leasing company. She requested they check the insurance on the vehicle. Result. This came back as insured to Paul Bell, 12 Orchard Court, Dundee.
Great. Now they had an address for him.

She contacted Marks immediately. 'Brilliant' said Marks.

0700 hours, Friday 6th April. All teams were ready and in position. DC Crighton was nervously sitting in the passenger seat whilst DC Mason was in the driver's seat. They had been tasked with identifying Bell as he makes his way to his car.

Unknown to him there was a three-man arrest team, kitted up in public order gear, waiting in an unmarked van ready to deal with whatever he had in store for them.

There was also a dog handler nearby should he try and run.

They (Marks and Black) had decided it was far safer to allow Bell to be in the open where they could see if he is armed rather than attend at his house where he knew the layout and where, if any, weapons would be.

0745 hours, 'Go, Go, Go' shouted Crighton through the radio.

She'd sighted Bell. Dressed in a suit with a black briefcase in his left hand and car keys in his right.

He was walking to his car when the van doors swung open and three police officers in riot gear jumped out shouting 'Police show me your hands' as they were running towards him, getting their hands on him and handcuffing his hands behind his back before he could work out what was going on.

It's fair to say that he never stood a chance of trying to resist arrest or put up a fight.

'Have you got anything on you shouldn't have?' asked one of the officers in riot gear.

'No' came the reply. 'What's going on?'

Marks had caught up with the officers and Bell.

'Paul Bell' said Marks

'Yeah'

'I'm detaining you for the murder of Jill Williams.'

As Marks was cautioning him, they sized each other up. Marks was thinking is this really the guy wanted for three murders. He's tall, stocky, clean shaven, but he seemed an unassuming character. A guy you'd think would be more suited to serving you at the local post office than one that was capable of raping and murdering three people. Bell declined to comment.

They searched him and found nothing of consequence on him.

He was placed in the back of an unmarked police car with two of the officers in riot gear. It was a tight fit, but that suited the officers because it meant there was less chance of Bell trying anything.

Even though he was handcuffed, it wouldn't be the first time someone has escaped their cuffs. Some people can willingly dislocate their thumb and wriggle out of the cuffs whilst others had hands that were that skinny that if the cuffs weren't placed in the smallest setting, they'd literally fall off them.

When they arrived at Police Headquarters cops were looking out of almost every window. Everyone wanted to see what a serial killer looked like.

Once they booked him through the custody suite, they placed him in a cell until his solicitor had been informed and was in attendance.

He was given a paper suit, all his clothes taken from him, and he was placed in an observation cell as procedure dictated. This is in order to keep an eye on him so that he doesn't do himself any harm as the dawn realisation hits him where he is and why he's there.

Whilst they awaited his solicitor, they took DNA samples from him. Marks had spoken to the manager of the Forensic labs in order to expedite the comparison between the samples taken from Bell and the ones collected from the three murder scenes.

Marks was also in the process of finishing off his interview plan for the interview with Bell, that he and Thompson would be conducting.

Bell's solicitor was downstairs at the public enquiry office.

Whilst they were doing this. DS Laws was collecting the search warrant for his house. Laws and a search team consisting of four searchers and a scribe. That way every find is corroborated, and the time/date and location of the find is documented in order that there is no dubiety regarding the items found.

The search would be conducted slowly and precisely.

However, it didn't take long for Laws to contact Marks with an update.

'Just wanted you to know before you go and interview Bell that we've found 6 pairs of women's panties in one of his drawers in the bedroom' said Laws.

'Brilliant. Keep at it and let me know if you find anything else'
'Ok sir'.

INTERVIEW WITH BELL

Marks and Thompson began to interview Bell about the Williams murder first simply because this is the murder for which he was detained due to him fitting the description of a male thought to have been responsible for the murder who was seen near to the locus at the time it is thought the crime was committed.

Marks' experience told him that they were in for a long night.

Although he had never interviewed a serial killer before he knew that they rarely admit their crimes and they rarely show remorse. He could recall a serial killer in America who had raped and killed thirteen women denying committing the murders despite evidence to the contrary. A forensic scientist had calculated that it was a seventy-eight trillion to one chance that he hadn't raped and killed the women. This was since his semen was found on twelve of the thirteen victims and fibres from the clothing of these victims being found on him. Despite this the man to this day, still claims to be innocent.

True to Marks' first thoughts, Bell denied knowing Elaine Dawson and Jill Williams. He denied ever being in their homes and stated he didn't know where either of the streets they lived in was. He did admit however knowing Alison Trent through the Krav Maga classes but denied being in her home or having anything to do with her murder.

Marks and Thompson were happy with this though because it meant if his DNA was present at any of the scenes, he wouldn't be able to explain that if he'd never been there before. Although Marks and Thompson both noticed that Bell's demeanour never changed at any point throughout the interview. This didn't go unnoticed by Black either. They believed they had either got the wrong man or that they were dealing with a psychopath. Both their experiences in the police told them it was the latter. Bell was a psychopath.

They knew however this would mean he, like a lot of psychopaths was intelligent, manipulative, calculating and narcissistic. He had no comprehension of anyone else's feeling. Everything was matter of fact with him. He had no cares in the world.

Although he wasn't admitting anything to them, they were positive that the DNA found in each of the murder scenes would come back to Bell. Also that the lady's underwear Laws, and the search team had found in his house would be forensically linked to the deceased women. Of course they asked him about this, but he said nothing.

Both Marks and Thompson knew it was him, they just needed a positive result from the DNA.
Several things bothered Marks about the murders though.

Such as, how did he enter Elaine Dawson's building if he wasn't seen on camera? Unless he lay in wait for her, entering the building prior to the time the cctv review started and assuming it wasn't missed.

How did he need to use a taser or stun gun? Bell was big, strong and skilled, he wouldn't have had a problem with any of the victims. Also what connected the victims? Why did he choose them?

He also wondered if they were his first killings. But surely if he had killed before using the same MO (Modus Operandi) then HOLMES would have picked up on it.

They decided to place him back in his cell whilst they regrouped, gathered their thoughts and decided how to progress. Hopefully the DNA result will be back in a few hours.

They were a momentary silence when the phone rang, a few people jumped because they were that on edge, Marks picked it up. Everyone in the office stopped doing what they had been doing, they knew the importance of this call. 'It's Forensics' said Marks to a packed audience. The voice on the other end of the line said 'The DNA sample taken from Bell was compared to the DNA obtained from all three murder scenes. It's a match to Paul Bell's. 'YESSSSSSS' shouted Marks. 'We've got him'

Cheering and cries of 'Yes' were heard throughout the office. Everyone was congratulating each other on catching a monster and a job well done.

'Thanks for that' said Marks.

He didn't have to tell everyone. They knew and he could see they were all happy. He phoned DS Laws to tell her the good news and see how they were getting on.

'You must be psychic. I was just about to phone you' said Laws 'Have you found something?' 'Yeah. You're not going to believe this.' Marks was still grinning from ear to ear, thinking he was about to get more good news.

'We've found fingers in his freezer'
'Brilliant' said Marks
'But'
'But…...but what?' asked Marks 'Well apparently, he cut off 20 fingers from the three murders, didn't he?'
'Yes, that's right'
'Well we've found a freezer drawer full. There must be about twice that many'

Marks' elation evaporated. People in the office could tell something wasn't right. Marks' expression went from smiling to disbelief.

'So there could be more victims?'
'There has to be' said Laws. 'I'll get back to you when we count them, but I reckon there's roughly 40-50 fingers in here. Oh and sorry to be the bearer of bad news but we haven't found any boots or shoes that have blood on them or that appear to have the same pattern as the partial footprint found at Jill Williams' flat.'

'Ok. Keep me updated'

'Sorry sir. What did you phone for?' 'Oh sorry. I was going to say the DNA from all the murders has come back as Paul Bell's'.

'Brilliant. Even if he has killed more people at least he's off the streets now.'

'Yeah. Good point. Keep me updated'. 'Ok'

Thompson spoke 'That didn't sound too good. What's up?'

Marks told them about the search team finding more fingers than they were hoping to find and about them not finding any boots to match the partial footprint found at Williams' flat.

The mood of the entire office had come crashing down.

Marks went along to Black's office to give him the news. Black however, was more positive than most. They'd got their man. There was nothing they could do now for the victims except try and get justice for them.

Marks knew he was right but couldn't help feeling dejected. However, he couldn't let Bell see he was dejected because it was time for another interview. This time they would be required to speak to him about any other murders he may have committed.

Not that he thought for a minute he would tell them anything. Bell liked the power. The power of knowing exactly what he did and to who.

CHAPTER 25

Marks and Thompson went in for another round with Bell. They stated that during the search of his property, police had recovered 45 fingers which had been found in his freezer.

'How many more people have you killed?' asked Marks. Bell's solicitor told him not to answer that.

Bell said nothing just smiled. Marks wanted to grab him by the head and smash it into the table until the smile disappeared from his face.

I know what will wipe the smile off your face, thought Marks. 'You said earlier that you didn't know Elaine Dawson or Jill Williams, in fact you said you didn't even know where the streets they lived in were. But after we put you back in your cell, we received the results of the DNA comparison of your DNA and the DNA we found at all three murder scenes, and it's a match.
How do you explain that?'

Bell shrugged his shoulders, smiled and said, 'can't be mine unless you put it there'.

Marks kept his cool, although he was finding it more difficult with each passing minute he spent in Bell's company.

'Did you kill Elaine Dawson?'
'No'
'Did you kill Alison Trent?'
'No'
'Did you kill Jill Williams?'
'No. I've never killed anyone in my life' said a smiling Bell.
Marks changed tactics. He asked Bell about his childhood and his relationship with his mother. Marks and Thompson saw Bell react for the first time. His eyes opened wide, his nostrils flared, and his fists tightened up.

'Paul, I'm sure your mum was great, all mums are great. They're always there for you and no matter what you do they'll always protect you.

'Was that what your mum was like?' asked Marks.
'No', said Bell, staring right at Marks. He'd clearly hit a nerve with this.
'What makes you say that?'

'She abandoned me after my dad died' Marks thought, great, keep him talking.
'Why what did she do?' Marks knew she'd sent him to live with his uncle. DC Fyffe had put this in the email to them.

'She sent me to live with my uncle while she drunk herself into an early grave.'
'That must have been a rough time with your father dying and your mum sending you to live with your uncle.
How did this make you feel?'
'How do you think it made me feel, fucking angry'
'What did you do to get rid of the anger?'
'I burnt things.
'What did you burn?'
'Everything'
'Even buildings?'
'No. Well yeah. Just one. Some factory'
'How did you do it?'
'Can't remember'
'Sure you can. Think back. Did you soak the place in petrol first, then light it? I'll bet you watched it burn as well, did you?'
'Don't answer that' said his solicitor. Bell was letting his guard down. He ignored the advice given to him by his solicitor. 'Yeah, we did it and watched from the hill opposite the factory'
'Who was with you?'
'No one'
'You said we. Who was with you?'
'No one'
How did that make you feel, watching the fire?'
'Great. It was good seeing it burn' Bell now had a fixed look on his face and a weird smile, like he was reliving the moment.
'You also enjoyed hurting animals, did you?'
'Yeah. I killed my guinea pigs. They were annoying me'
'What were they doing?' 'Nothing just sitting there. I got bored so I killed them.'
'How did you kill them' 'I stabbed them, then I cut them up. Mum wasn't happy. But they were boring anyway.'
'Did you kill any other animals?'
'Yeah. Cats. I don't like cats'
'How did that make you feel?'
'Yeah ok'
'Did it not bother you killing animals?'
'Nah'
'Was it the same killing the women?'
'Don't answer that' said his solicitor once again. But once again he was ignored. Bell was staring straight ahead. He was reliving the murders. He had a weird smile of satisfaction and pleasure on his face. His head tilted to one side.

'It was better. Coz I could look into their eyes and see they were in pain'
'What were you doing to them?'
'Releasing them from the pain of this world'
'What did you do to them?'

'A broad grin came across his face. He looked straight through Marks 'I squeezed their scrawny little necks, while I fucked them'. He closed his eyes at this point. 'It was so good'

A chill ran through Marks. This was as cold a killer as he'd ever come across. But he had stay focused.

'Is that what you did to all of them?'
'Yeah' said Bell still smiling.
'Why did you cut the fingers off?' asked Marks
'I had to show them I was in charge'
'Why did you cut off both of Jill Williams' hands?' 'She needed taught a lesson.'
'Why what did she do?'
'She punched.....' Marks got the impression he was about to say a name but managed to stop short of saying it.

Marks asked, 'who did she punch?'
Then as if someone had clicked their fingers he came around. 'I'm saying nothing'
'Ok that's fine Paul' said Marks
'Just one last question. How did you get into Elaine Dawson's building without being noticed?'

Again he smiled 'aha' said Bell putting his finger up to his nose, like it was a trade secret. 'I've said enough. Now I want to go back to my cell'.

Marks and Thompson tried their best to ask him a few more questions, but he wouldn't even acknowledge them.

They arrested him before presenting him at the charge bar and giving him his rights as an arrested person and placing him back in his cell.

Marks and Thompson went to update Black. As they were walking Marks said to Thompson
'Do you think he did this on his own?'
'I don't know' said Thompson, because he was about to say a name, at least I think he was, when he said Jill Williams punched someone'
'Yeah. I thought so too. Plus when you consider what Dr Dempster said about Jill Williams' fingers being cut off by someone who was left-handed. Did you notice he signed his name on the arrest forms with the pen in his right hand'?
'I did" said Thompson.
They updated Black.

'Great result. Great result' said Black. 'Of course we'll need to try and track down whoever these fingers are, but that could take time.'

They told Black about their gut feeling that there was maybe someone helping Bell judging by what he said. He told them to investigate it but to bear in mind they had just managed to obtain the confession of a serial killer.

He was right they thought, but Marks couldn't stop thinking someone's hiding something.

Marks contacted DC Fyffe. He asked him to the best of his knowledge could he remember if Mathew Davie had any friends or an accomplice in any of his crimes.

Fyffe recalled that police thought there were two boys that set the factory on fire and that Mathew was not actually the instigator of this. But they couldn't get him to give up his mate's name. To this day he doesn't know who it was. He couldn't remember the name of the boy that was friends with him for a short time before moving away.

Marks thanked him for his information because without it they may not have caught him and subsequently charged him with three murders.

He never found out how he managed to enter Elaine Dawson's building.

Marks stopped into a garage on the way home for petrol. After filling up his car he went to pay for the petrol. As he approached the checkout, he saw Scott Young paying for some juice and a sandwich.

'Hi sir' said Young on seeing Marks.
Marks said 'Hi' and noticed his nose looked broken and he was sporting a black eye. He thought nothing of it and paid for his petrol.

Although Marks had his hands full with the murders he had not forgotten about Sarah Robertson and the fact that despite her modest earnings as a primary school teacher, she owned two flats
roughly valued at ninety thousand pounds each and a top of the range Mercedes.

He had passed this investigation onto other CID officers. They had applied for and had obtained a search warrant from the court based on Robertson appearing to have a criminal lifestyle from which she has gained from.

They attended at Robertson's flat. The one across from the first flat that police had spoken to her in.

They traced Robertson in her first flat and made her aware of what they were about to do. She let them into the flat. Not that she had a choice, because if they were to break down the door, she would be liable for the damages. She allowed them entry.

Inside the flat was a massive flat screen OLED tv, that DS Burns, who oversaw the enquiry, thought was worth several thousand pounds. There was an expensive laptop, designer clothes, designer handbags and shoes.

Unfortunately for Robertson there were receipts and price tags on various items which indicated she was living way beyond her means.

However, the biggest regret Robertson would have was when police found her safe, hidden behind some shoes in her designer wardrobes. The safe contained £18,000 in cash.

Not only did police seize the electrical equipment, designer clothes and shoes but also the money.
Judging by the amount of money police had seized, the quantity and quality of the goods taken also, Robertson had clearly been in business for a long time.

She would see the inside of a court before too long, thought Marks.

CHAPTER 26

Suddenly Conor awoke…..how did he not get that straight away, of course it all made sense now… entry to the building, the broken nose…..I'll bet if they looked at his footwear it'll be his footprint at the side of the Jill Williams' bed. He was left-handed too. Damn. You would've figured this out ages ago in your youth, he thought. He thought about texting Black but then he looked at the time and realised it was twenty pasts two in the morning. I'll tell him in the morning.

She sat upright, awoken from what she thought was a horrific nightmare. It was a nightmare was it…...oh no…. oh no…..she held her head in her hands, how could you make that mistake. She realised it wasn't a nightmare. She realised she had got her dates mixed up. Must've been with the grief. He's done it. She felt sick to her stomach, a chill ran through her bones. She knew she was sharing a house with a killer.

But she was his mum. He wouldn't hurt her….would he? I'm his mum and I must protect him after all that's what mum's do, they protect their young. Even when he went through a phase of starting fires when he was young and got in with a bad crowd., I looked after him. That's why they moved away from Aberdeen after all. She was thinking the words but why was she terrified?

She got up. Her head was telling her to go and confront him, but her body was saying get out. Her head won this battle she put her nightgown on and went to his bedroom. She knocked. No answer.

She knocked again. Still no answer. Very slowly she opened the door and entered.

He was gone. On his bed lay a letter he'd left for her…..

MUM it said on the envelope. She opened it…. tears roll down her face as she read how he along with his friend had done something awful and that as much as he loved her, he couldn't stay. He wanted to tell somebody the truth because it was killing him knowing what he'd done and how he'd let her down. He'd let everybody down, especially his daughter Katie. He wished he was born someone else. He hated what he'd become but he couldn't help himself.

He stated in the letter how he'd started having an affair with Elaine Dawson but that after a while she'd wanted more and had even threatened to tell Rachel (his wife) about the affair. So he arranged for her to be killed. He'd left her after having sex with her, only to return with Mathew Davie, (as soon as she saw that name, she knew he was the catalyst for Scott going off the rails).

Mathew told him the only way to shut her up was to kill her. But he couldn't do it. So Mathew did.

He tasered her as she opened the door, she most probably thought it was him.

He had let Mathew in the fire escape whilst he then left via the front door. That way it would give him an alibi because he would return to work and no one would see him enter the building.

Alison Trent was Mathew's idea. He did this by himself because he fancied her as soon as he seen her in the Krav Maga classes. But she never gave him the time of day because she felt there was something about him, she didn't like. Guess she was right.

The murder of Jill Williams was a Mathews idea too. He'd seen her walking home and decided she was next. No reason behind it. She was in the wrong place at the wrong time. I stood and watched him rape her. I was frozen with fear, stuck to the spot. Then he told me to cut her fingers off as punishment for punching and breaking my nose.

I didn't want to do it, but Mathew told me to do it and I was scared ….'she deserved it, how dare she punch you in the face' he said.
I can't go to prison. An ex-cop in prison. I wouldn't last a week.
Scott had gone...his passport was also missing.
She reported him missing in the morning.

However, later that day Marks' team received news that the partial boot print had come from a pair work boots police had recovered from Young's bedroom.

Marks suspected the blood on the hall walls was his too, but he would need further DNA tests carried out from items recovered from his home and blood found in the hall.

As they carried out further enquiry into Young's whereabouts it became apparent that the last person to see him was in fact DCI Conor Marks at the petrol station.

But Young had gone.

Meanwhile, everyone else went back to their normal lives. Neil Purvis, continued working as a concierge. Kevin Ferguson started dating Paula Crighton and they had decided to move in together. Marks was pleased with this because he liked Paula, she deserved to be with someone who treated her well.

Gordon Harvey and Sarah Robertson never spoke to one another after the police involvement. Of course, this was expected, especially after Harvey spilled the beans about her having two flats and this resulted in Robertson losing £18,000 in cash and over £100,000 in assets. The court's decision was that Robertson profited from her illegal activities to such an extent that she could only have gained these assets from prostitution.

That's it thought Marks. He had decided he was going to allow Kevin to be their mum's Power of Attorney. After all he had this disease to battle now and there was no way he could effectively look after his mother if he was about to struggle to look after himself.

Although he was aware the Neurologist said people decline at their own rate, he couldn't have his mother stay with him until he deteriorated before moving her away to stay with Kevin. He didn't like the idea of her staying with him, but he felt as if the choice had been made for him.

Later that night he phoned Kevin to let him know about his diagnosis and that he felt it best their mum stays with him. To be fair to Kevin he seemed gutted for Marks but agreed this seemed like the best decision for all concerned.

At least his mother was physically well after her move, albeit she was struggling to settle at night because her routine had changed.

However, Marks' mother deteriorated rapidly after initially settling in well with Marks' brother down south and unfortunately died a few weeks later from complications sustained from a bad fall.

As Marks reflected on his last case as Senior Investigating Officer, his physical health remained the same whilst he was battling to overcome the psychological aspects of Parkinson's by keeping his mind and body occupied through keeping fit and continuing working.

He found he could still do all the things he used to be able to do but that if he was having a bad day, then it may take him 3 or four times longer than normal. The recovery time from physical exertions had increased significantly. But Marks was staying positive. Of course it was helped by the fact his relationship with Susan was going from strength to strength.

There was no such thing however as a normal day for him, but he was always of the opinion that whilst he was living in hope of a cure there were people living with conditions that were worse than his. So count yourself lucky Marks and appreciate what you've got whilst you have it because life is short so enjoy it while you can.

Although the police hadn't had someone work for them who was suffering with Parkinson's, Marks found them to be very accommodating. In fact he thought they were superb in their handling of the situation. He couldn't have asked any more of them. They had someone from occupational health come up and assess his office and see if there was anything, they could do to assist him. They got him a new chair and a footstool. They even offered him a new office on the ground floor, in case he struggled with stairs. However, he accepted the new chair and footstool but didn't want to much upheaval and so would remain where he was now.

However hard this battle with Parkinson's was, he was determined to fight it every day. He knew some days Parkinson's would win, but he wasn't going to let it ruin who he was, or what he wanted to do. Yes, things may take longer for him to do, and yes it may take him longer to recover, but it wasn't going to get the better of him. He has always been and will always be a fighter.

He'd had a tough time recently, with his mother dying and the diagnosis, but he remained hopeful for the future. He had also started a relationship with Susan. She was a physiotherapist at the local hospital and had been given the job of assessing Marks' needs, now that he was suffering from Parkinson's. She was a few years younger than him and had no family, only an ex-husband. They had only been in a relationship for a few weeks, but Marks was very happy.

Although he often thought about what Parkinson's would mean for him and Susan in the future, he simply took each day as it came. Every night finished the same however, with him saying Fuck you Parkinson's.

TO BE CONTINUED………

Printed by Amazon Italia Logistica S.r.l.
Torrazza Piemonte (TO), Italy